# Raven's Haven

## Book One
## *Fighting for Forgiveness*

# *Cassidy K. O'Connor*

Raven's Haven – Fighting for Forgiveness

Copyright 2019 Cassidy K. O'Connor

Published by Celtic Hearts Press

Cover Art by B Creative Designs

Formatting by Celtic Formatting

# Dedication

Far too often women feel alone when faced with their greatest fears, regrets, or shortcomings. I hope you come to find solace with one of the women at Raven's Haven and know that you aren't alone. Every woman deserves to find her tribe of supporters, her own haven. If you haven't yet, I hope Raven's Haven will help until you do.

To my daughter, Kelsie, I wish I could have made the world a better, safer place for you and all young women to grow up in. Women are the future, standing shoulder to shoulder we can make it better for the next generation.

# Acknowledgements

Thank you to my mom, and sisters for always being there for my late-night texts asking questions and opinions.

Thank you to Char and Sarah, you're the beta readers I never knew were missing from my life. I am so glad you were loaned to me, I'm grateful for all of your input.

# One

Mason's skin crawled as he watched over the girl sitting alone in the corner booth. She was twirling a lock of hair through her fingers as she read a book and nibbled slowly on her dinner. She wasn't even aware of the leers the creep was giving her.

The rest of her hair was thrown up in a lazy bun on top of her head. Her arms were so thin Mason was sure she didn't have any muscles. With a single glance, you could tell she was the introverted type.

She finally finished her meal and walked up to the register to pay. The piece of shit watching her threw money on the counter and walked out of the restaurant. Mason had no doubt he was up to something. He waited until she left before he paid his bill and followed her out.

The muggy night air was a stark contrast from the frigid café. He scanned the street and saw the girl cross to his right. As expected, a minute later the greasy looking thug popped out of a side street and started to follow her. Mason walked at a distance, never taking his eyes off of them. He wasn't convinced yet that the guy was going to do something to the girl but he wanted to be close in case he did.

As she got her car door open, the guy launched himself at her and tried to shove her into the passenger seat. Mason kicked into high gear and got to them just as she let out her first scream.

The knife in the attacker's hand reflected off the street lamp above them as Mason reached in and yanked him out of the car. The confusion and shock on his face gave Mason the time he needed to knock the knife out of his hand. In the thug's enraged state, it was smarter to step back and let him lunge first.

His sloppy moves made it too easy for Mason to step to his left and knee him in the groin. As soon as he dropped to his knees, Mason punched him in the nose and enjoyed watching the attacker fall back into oblivion.

Mason pulled his phone out of his pocket and called 911. He gave the operator their location and said he would wait until the police arrived. He glanced into the car and saw the girl still huddled in the passenger seat. She looked so frail with her knees pulled up to her chest, cradling her arms and sobbing.

He kneeled on the driver's seat and held his hands up to show her he didn't have a weapon. "Miss are you okay? The police are on their way, stay in the car until they get here."

She looked at him with huge, blue eyes overflowing with tears as she reached out a shaking hand. He noticed the blood and cursed for not realizing she might have gotten hurt in their scuffle. A long gash ran down the length of her forearm. He ripped his shirt off and wrapped her arm. Relief flooded him as he saw the first police car arrive. She was in shock and he wasn't sure how to help her.

Mason grabbed her quivering chin and made her look at him. "I'll be right back. I'm going to let the police know you need medical attention."

He climbed out with his hands raised. The cops approached with their guns drawn. He knew it didn't look good that he had blood on both hands and was half naked.

"I'm the good guy. I found this guy with a knife trying to jump the woman in the car." He gave the unconscious man a kick in the ribs for good measure, then pointed at the weapon still on the ground. "The guy got her with the knife before I could get him off her. She's not critical but she needs someone to look at it."

The officer closest to him rushed around the car and asked the girl to unlock the passenger door. While they talked, he watched as the other cop rolled the guy over and handcuffed him. Mason realized he must have had a lot more rage than he thought since the perv was still out cold.

The cop left him like that and looked in the car at his partner. "You need help?"

The officer was putting pressure on the wound, "I've already called in requesting two ambulances, she'll be fine until then."

Mason glanced down the road as he heard sirens in the distance. Red and blue lights shining through the darkness came towards them.

The car door next to him shut dragging Mason's attention back to the waiting officer. "I need to get your statement."

As he finished his side of the story the ambulance rolled up. The paramedics split between the real victim and the trash still on the ground. They flashed a light in his eyes and finally got him to wake up. The cop helped him stand then took him behind the squad car to separate him from his victim.

Mason was relieved when the girl managed to climb out of the car on her own, albeit with shaky legs, and walked to the ambulance.

He spotted her purse sticking out from under the car. He picked it up and walked it over to the female police officer and handed it to her. "How's she doing?"

"She's going to need some stitches, but other than that she seems okay. She has you to thank, it could have been worse."

Mason let out a deep breath of air, "I'm just glad I was in the right place at the right time."

One of the paramedics walked over and handed Mason a bottle with clear liquid in it. "Here's some saline so you can wash your hands off."

Mason took it gladly; the blood had started to dry and flake. Knowing it belonged to the girl made him eager to get it off, he didn't want the reminder that he was once again too late.

"She's ready to go and asked if you would be willing to ride along with her."

He glanced into the ambulance and locked eyes with her. He could see the fear and shock in them. "Sure, I'll stay with her."

He climbed into the back and sat where the paramedic told him to. He felt awkward sitting shirtless so he crossed his arms trying to fade into the background more. He watched as the paramedic fiddled with her arm and took down notes. She kept glancing up at him out of the corner of her eyes.

As soon as he felt the ambulance moving he cleared his throat, "My name's Mason. I'm sorry you were hurt. I should have gotten to him before he grabbed you."

For a few seconds she didn't say anything. Finally, she whispered. "Thank you for being there, Mason. I didn't even notice him. If it weren't for you..."

Her soft, melodic voice trailed off as fear flashed in her eyes again. He could tell she was playing out scenarios in her head. He needed to get her to stop picturing all those horrible possibilities. "It's okay. Don't think about that right now. Why don't you tell me your name?"

Her voice shook, "Mia."

"That is a lovely name, Mia. I saw you in the café earlier reading. What book was it?"

She looked at him sheepishly, "You're going to laugh if I tell you."

He feigned a look of shock and outrage. "I would never laugh!" He got a smile out of her, which released some of the tension in his shoulders that he didn't realize was there.

"I was reading the final Harry Potter book for probably the millionth time."

"A geek, I can respect that. My sister loved those books, but I admit I never read them."

It was her turn to feign shock and outrage.

The paramedic got her attention. "I'm going to give you something for the pain. You might start feeling sleepy." He waited for her to nod before pushing the clear liquid into the IV sticking out of her uninjured arm.

Less than a minute later her eyes unfocused, and her breathing slowed down. "Wow, this stuff works fast."

The paramedic laughed softly, "It usually helps if you close your eyes. You won't get as dizzy or nauseous."

She reached her good hand out to Mason. He took it and held it between his hoping to get some warmth into her. Her bones were as small and fragile as he thought they might be. She was lucky the guy didn't break anything while they were fighting.

Mia's jaw tensed as she tried to hold back a yawn, "If I fall asleep will you stay with me?"

His sister's image popped into his head, he shook the feelings aside and agreed. He was never going to turn away someone that needed help again. As her eyes drifted closed, he heard her whisper something about large muscles and nice abs. The paramedic looked at him with one eyebrow raised. He tried not to blush as he shrugged.

The paramedic reached into a drawer and pulled out a small blanket. "You probably don't want to go into the ER like that."

Mason was grateful for the coverage, he really did feel out of place being less clothed than everyone else.

The ambulance pulled up to the hospital and they were sucked into a whirlwind of activity. As the paramedic pulled the gurney out. Mason was forced to let go of her hand for a minute.

She bolted upright, her gaze darting around, "Where's Mason, where'd he go?"

Multiple nurses stood in the doorway waiting for the stretcher to be brought in. "Don't worry sweetie your boyfriend is right here. He'll follow behind you, but first we need to get you checked out." The nurse looked up from the chart to give him a reassuring smile and waved at him to follow behind. "Let us get her settled then we'll get you something to clean up with."

The cops from the scene were already waiting in the room they wheeled Mia into and gave the doctors the rundown of what happened. Mason hung outside the room, unsure what he was supposed to do.

He leaned against the wall and stared up at the ceiling. His only memories from a hospital were bad ones and he didn't want to look around and see other people in pain. He didn't want the reminder of what he went through.

The cops left Mia's room and nodded at him as they walked over to the nurse's station.

He went back to staring at the ceiling and waited for someone to give him something to do instead of standing there in limbo.

Once the nurses and doctor had assessed she had no life-threatening injuries, a nurse came out to tell him they were going to take her up for an x-ray and she'd be back in fifteen minutes. He stood outside the door and waited for them to finish prepping her.

Someone cleared their throat behind him. He turned and spotted two young women in scrubs smiling up at him. "Hi there, we heard you rescued her tonight." They glanced at Mia, and then back to him.

"You're quite the hero, aren't you?" They leaned in and one of them laid her hand on his arm. He was starting to feel trapped and uncomfortable, so he looked around for an escape.

The nurse who had met them at the ambulance came out and shooed the girls away. "Don't mind those two, they think they are on *Grey's Anatomy* or something. Let me get you a shirt and that might calm them down a bit."

He was grateful when the nurse came back with a blue scrub top. As he slipped it over his head, they wheeled Mia by. Her eyes were unfocused and he could tell she was still high on whatever drug they had given her.

"Going to get my picture taken...I'll be back in a jiff." She giggled and gestured forward with her good arm. "The paparazzi await."

He chuckled and watched her till she was out of sight.

A crash to his right caught his attention. One of the cop's stopped writing his report to go investigate. Mason walked over and peeked inside the room. Mia's attacker was fighting a nurse, who was trying to bandage his still bleeding nose.

His wrists were handcuffed to the bed, he pulled against them as he thrashed around. "Settle down or I'll cuff your ankles to the bed too." The cop threatened.

Mason couldn't help the smug smile on his face knowing he caused the man's pain.

He glanced around at the otherwise empty hall. Not sure what else to do, he went into Mia's room. The recliner in the corner looked comfortable. He settled into the chair when one of the officer's came in and asked him to verify and sign his version of the incident.

"The perp is done so we're going to take him out of here before she gets back. She seemed out of it, so she may not remember I told her I put her purse on the rack under her gurney."

"I'll make sure she gets it. Were you able to reach anyone to come get her?" He didn't notice he was biting his nail.

She shook her head, "Her parents live in Kansas and asked if they should fly here. I told them that probably wasn't necessary but they should wait to hear from Mia after she saw the doctor." She glanced down at her phone before looking back at him. "They want to speak with her and find out what she wants them to do."

Mason was disappointed to hear she didn't have anyone coming to be with her. "Thanks, I'll have her call them when she's a little more lucid. If she needs me to, I'll give her a ride home. She shouldn't take a cab tonight."

"I'm sure she will be grateful for your help. She really is lucky you came along when you did. This guy has a prior assault conviction, so you can guess what his plans were."

He couldn't help rolling his eyes, disgusted the guy had still been out on the streets to hurt someone else. They shook hands, then he settled back into the recliner to play on his phone while he waited for Mia to return. Within minutes, an x-ray technician rolled her back into the room.

"Hey, my hero is still here. Nurse Shelley, have you met Mason? He saved my life tonight."

She leaned closer to the nurse, and said in a stage-whisper, "Can you complain to whoever gave him a shirt to put on?"

Nurse Shelley smiled at him as she locked the wheels on the gurney. Mason tried to hide his grin.

"It's very nice to meet you, Mason." She turned back to her patient. "Now I want you to rest until the doctor comes back in."

Mia gave the nurse a lazy salute and flopped her arm back onto the bed. Mason was concerned with how big a dose they had given her. He imagined she seemed the type who would be mortified tomorrow if she remembered any of this.

She closed her eyes and sighed. He sat there awkwardly, not sure what to say next. He was saved when he heard adorable little snores coming from her. He sat back and stared around the room. It had plain white walls, a blue curtain to pull across the glass doors, and a sink in the corner with a T.V. mounted on the wall above it. He looked around the bed for the remote, when he heard buzzing. He poked around and found it was coming from her purse. He peeked in and saw her phone lit up, he grabbed it and sat back quickly so she didn't think he was digging around.

The screen showed a picture of a man in his fifties with gray hair, with "Daddy" written underneath. He could imagine the man was worried sick, so he decided to answer.

"Hello sir, this is Mason."

An angry voice on the other end of the line yelled back at him, "Who the hell are you and why are you answering my baby girl's phone?"

"I'm not sure how much the police told you. I'm the one that saw Mia get attacked and I stepped in to help her. She asked me to stay at the hospital while she gets checked out." He gulped for air, not realizing he had tried to cram that entire spiel out in one breath.

Mason heard a heavy sigh on the other end of the line, "Well okay...thank God for you. The police didn't give us your name, is she okay?

We told her not to move away. We warned her cities can be dangerous."

Mason raised his eyebrows at that last part. Savannah was a city sure, but not really considered a dangerous place to live.

"They took her for an x-ray and she's sleeping right now. I don't think anything is broken. She'll need stitches though."

"The police said you beat the tar out of the guy?"

Mason smiled smugly into the phone. "Yes sir, I broke his nose and made him rethink his ability to have children."

The older man laughed loudly then sobered, "Atta boy, thanks again for being there when I wasn't."

Right then the doctor walked in. Mason could hear the shame in her father's voice and felt bad for having to hang up instead of offering words of comfort. "Sir, the doctor is here to see her now. I'll have her call you as soon as she's done."

"Okay, take care of our girl."

"Will do, bye." He hung up the phone and reached out to shake the doctor's waiting hand. She was young, blonde, and had one hell of a handshake.

"Hi, I'm Dr. Chambers. Let's go ahead and wake Mia up and have a chat." She leaned over Mia and rubbed her good arm. "Mia, can you wake up and talk to me?"

She called her name a couple of times before Mia finally opened her eyes and tried to focus on the face in front of her.

"Hi Mia, I'm Dr. Chambers. We're going to sit your bed up so we can talk."

Mia nodded but didn't say anything.

The doctor pushed some buttons and helped Mia adjust to a sitting position. "Your x-rays are back and I didn't see any fractures. The cut is deep though, so I've paged plastics to come and sew you up. After that, you should be good to head home. You are going to want to take the pain pills religiously for the next day or so. Do you have someone that can stay with you?"

Mia glanced at Mason out of the corner of her eye, then shook her head no. "I just moved here a couple of months ago and haven't made any friends yet."

Mason sat forward, "If you want, I have a female friend who you would get along with well. She'll be happy to come hang with us for the night and we'll make sure you are taken care of."

She studied his face for a few seconds. "Well, you already stopped someone from hurting me and gave up your Friday night to babysit me so I assume you aren't a bad guy." She gave a shy smile, "If your friend is available I would appreciate the company."

He stood and pulled his phone out of his pocket. "I'm going to step outside and give her a call. I'll be right back."

In the hall, he scrolled through his contact list for Mary's number and gave her a call. On the first ring, she answered, as he expected.

"Hello?"

"Hi Mary, It's Mason from Raven's Haven." The two nurses from earlier waved at him. He smiled, then turned towards Mia's room. He didn't want to give them any ideas that he was interested.

"Oh, hi Mason. Is everything okay? It's late."

He looked at the clock on the wall and realized it was only ten-thirty on a Friday night. Mary was a homebody. He should have thought of that before bothering her. "I'm sorry for calling so late. I have a favor to ask, though. I stopped an attack on a girl and I'm at the ER with her now. The doctor doesn't want her staying alone tonight and she doesn't have anyone else. Would you mind coming to pick us up and stay the night with me at her place? I think she'll be more comfortable if another female is there."

"Absolutely." She exclaimed.

He knew it wasn't that she was happy about another person's misfortune, it was more that she was happy to be needed. From everything he knew about her she didn't have any family and friends in the area so she seemed pretty lonely. "Are you at St. Michael's or Presbyterian Memorial?"

"We're at St. Michaels. She still needs to get stitched up so you have time to pack a bag."

"Okay, I will be there in twenty minutes. I'll sit in the parking lot till you text that you are ready to go."

"Thanks, Mary, see you soon." As he turned to head back in the room, he almost bumped into another doctor. The man waved him in first and waited until Mason was back in the recliner.

"Hi Mia, I'm Dr. Candito. I heard you need some stitches."

Mia and Mason took turns shaking his hand, then watched as he started opening tools on a tray.

He pulled the stool up to the bed and settled her arm on the tray. Mason's stomach pitched as the doctor peeled the bandages off her arm and inspected the wound. He didn't know anything about injuries like this, but the cut looked jagged.

"I'm going to give you a few injections with lidocaine to numb around the area."

Mia took a deep breath and steadied her arm. Each needle piercing her skin looked like it hurt. Mason was impressed, however, that she never made a sound. The doctor wrapped the bandage back around her arm and stood up. "Okay let's give that a few minutes, then I'll come back to clean and stitch it."

Mason waited until he left the room before talking again. "You took that like a champ. Did it hurt?"

Mia hugged her arm against her chest as she laughed. "Like a mother."

Mason chuckled. "While you were asleep your dad called. I figured he was probably pretty worried about you so I answered and spoke to him. I hope that's okay?"

She nodded, "That was probably for the best or he would already be in the car on his way here."

He held her phone up toward her. "He'd probably like to hear from you. Are you up for a call now?"

"Yeah, let's get this over with." After she took the phone, he sat back in the recliner again. She took a deep breath and dialed him up.

"Hi, dad...yeah, I'm okay. They just numbed up my arm and the doctor is coming back to put the stitches in." She glanced at Mason again and then rolled her eyes. "Yes dad, he's still here." She paused again, "Yes, he and one of his friends are going to stay with me tonight." She rolled her eyes, "Of course, she's a girl." She mouthed sorry to Mason, "No Dad, I don't need you guys to come down here. I promise I'm okay."

Dr. Candito came back in the room and sat on his stool.

"Dad I need to go, the doctor is back. I'll call you guys tomorrow. Tell Mom I love her."

Mia handed Mason the phone and took a deep breath before putting her arm back on the tray.

The doctor took the bandages off and threw them away. He lifted her arm over a bucket and poured a bottle of saline over it. She sat calmly through the entire process.

"Okay Mia, time to sew you up. You might not want to watch."

She nodded and looked over at Mason. "So, Mason, is superhero your full-time job or do you do something else as well?"

The needle pierced her skin. Mason jerked his eyes away quickly before he got nauseous. "I'm no superhero...just lucky I was nearby when you needed help." He glanced back at her arm then quickly back at her, "I actually opened a gym last year." He was surprised when she gave him a look of disgust. "I'm guessing you aren't a fan of them?"

"I went to a gym once and felt like I was being ogled the entire time. There were way too many meatheads just showing off their muscles."

"I admit I used to be one of those meatheads. Not anymore, though. I realized the world wasn't as nice as I thought and I grew up. I think you would like my gym. It has an old time feel and I specialize in self-defense. Some of the classes are women only, and trust me, you would love the ladies who attend. The girl you're meeting tonight, Mary, is part of the class." It used to be hard for him to mention his old ways as it brought up thoughts of his sister. It got a little easier every day.

"So, you didn't just open your own gym for easy access to women?" Mia's cheeks pinkened, her eyes widened.

He assumed she didn't mean to say that out loud and the medicine was still affecting her. "I can see why you'd think that. Come to one of the classes and decide for yourself."

Dr. Candito cleared his throat to get their attention. "These stitches need to stay in for two weeks. I'm going to send home some supplies for you to use the first few days. One of the nurses will print out instructions on how to clean it. Call your primary care doctor's office tomorrow and make a follow-up appointment in 14 days."

Mason stood when the doctor did, shook his hand, and thanked him.

"No need to thank me, son. From what I hear you are the one to be thanked. Take care of her and make sure she gets home safe."

As he left, the nurse came in with her discharge paperwork and instructions. Once it was signed, he offered to hold her things for her.

He texted Mary that they were on their way out. "Tell me the truth, is this a good color for me?" He made a big deal of showing off her purse hanging from his shoulder. It felt good to hear her laugh, especially after the news he was about to give her.

"My friend is picking us up here, the police had to impound your car since it was the scene of the crime. Don't worry though, we'll stop at the pharmacy to fill your prescription and then get you home."

He glanced over at her, shocked to see tears running down her face. He pulled her to the side of the hallway and turned her to face him.

"Everything is going to be okay. Don't worry about your car or anything else tonight."

Her chin quivered, "I'm sorry, It's not only the car. I just can't believe I'm here and this is happening. When I got up this morning, I thought this would be another average day." She wiped the tears from her face and took a deep breath. "I'm fine, between the shock and the pain meds, I'm just not processing well."

"Come on, let's get you home."

He led her out the emergency room doors. Mary was standing next to her car waiting for them. He waved and brought Mia around to the passenger side where Mary was holding the door open.

"Mary, I'd like you to meet Mia. She is new in town and hasn't met many people yet. I think you two could be good friends."

They smiled shyly and waved to each other. He helped Mia in and handed her the seat belt buckle.

Once she was settled he closed the door and climbed in the back seat. "Thanks again for coming to get us."

Mary glanced back at him, "No problem, I'm always happy to help."

Mason buckled his seatbelt. "Alright, next stop is the pharmacy."

He leaned back and took stock of his evening. He'd been planning a quiet night at home. Something pushed him to go in to the restaurant he was walking by. Maybe it was his sister looking out for the girl and she sent him into that café to watch over her?

## Two

Mia stared out the window replaying the night in her head. Her mind stuck in a book caused her to miss the guy following her. She had barely managed a scream when he had pointed the knife at her.

A gentle touch on her shoulder made her jerk away. "Hey, are you okay? You are shaking and started breathing really fast."

Mia was pulled from her thoughts, she smiled sheepishly at Mary. "Sorry, yeah, just lost in thought."

They pulled up to the twenty-four-hour pharmacy and she was happy for the distraction. She didn't want to talk about that little episode.

Mia opened her car door and it was promptly shut again. She looked out the window to find Mason shaking his head at her. Mary rolled her window down.

"Just give me your insurance card and I'll take care of the rest. Is there anything else either of you want?"

Mary leaned over and asked for a bottle of sweet tea. Mia gave him her insurance card, sixty dollars, and asked for a red Gatorade. He plucked the card out of her hand, leaving the money behind. "Mason seriously, take my money."

He put his hands up, refusing to let her hand him anything else. "No, I owe you. It's my fault we're even here right now. If I had intervened sooner you wouldn't be hurt."

On that note, he turned and went inside. She shook her head and turned to Mary. "I would love to understand how he thinks any of this is his fault?"

Mary gave her a sad smile. "He blames himself for not protecting you."

Mia rolled her eyes, "Well, that's just idiotic."

"He can't help it. He went through a lot of stuff a few years ago and it really changed him. He'll tell you about it when he's ready, just keep in mind he's a lot more sensitive than he looks."

Her words intrigued Mia, like most readers, she enjoyed a good story and wanted to learn more about her mysterious rescuer.

Mary's phone buzzed, distracting her from her contemplation. "Hello? Okay, I'll tell her." She tossed her phone in the cup holder. "Mason said your script will be ready in ten minutes."

"Cool. Thanks again for giving up your night to help me. I guess I really need to start making friends if I'm going to stay here."

Mary beamed back at her, "Well you've got two now and if you come meet the others from our class, you will have a bunch more."

The idea of having a large group of friends made her yearn for something she didn't realize she wanted. "So, you guys are all really close?"

Mary shrugged, "We don't really hang out after class, but everyone in there has been through stuff, and I know I could call any of them for help and they would be there for me."

"They sound pretty awesome."

Mary turned in her chair to face Mia. "They are, you'll love them. We have class on Mondays, Wednesdays, and Saturdays. You should come and watch." Mary's excitement was calling to Mia, enticing her to give it a shot.

"Yeah, maybe when my arm is a little better, I will." She stared out her window unsure what else to say.

The silence didn't last long when Mason came out.

Mia whistled, "Wow, did you buy the whole store?"

His arms were loaded down with three bags. "I bought everything you might need tonight. I'll show you when we get to your house."

Mary pulled out of the parking lot and followed the GPS to her house. They pulled in the driveway, Mary's mouth dropped open. "Wow, this whole place is yours?"

"Yeah, my dad was not happy about me living on my own. He scoped out crime rates, neighborhood safety, and stuff, and I picked something in the areas he approved of. I drew the line when he tried to make me get a guard dog too."

"Must be nice to have someone care about you that much." Mary said wistfully.

They sat in awkward silence for a second. Mia didn't know how to respond. "I'm an only child and I moved out of state. I get how scary that is, his intentions are good, so I don't mind. Do your parents live in the area?"

Mason had already climbed out and opened her door for her. They got out and Mary collected her bag and locked the car before responding.

"My parents are a few towns over, we don't talk much. We have a difference of beliefs and they struggle to accept that I think differently than they do." She shrugged and walked towards the front door.

Surprised by her nonchalance she turned to see if Mason had a better relationship with his family. "What about you Mason? Are your parents in the area?"

"Yep." With that terse response, he walked towards the porch. There was definitely a backstory she was missing.

Mia's arm started throbbing again as she quickly made her way up the walkway and opened the door.

They followed her into the kitchen and unpacked the bags while she took a pain pill. Her eyes widened at the wide range of items they were setting down. He bought soda, Gatorade, water, a crossword book, a word search book, popcorn, chips, and surprisingly, cookie dough. She held it up to him with one eyebrow raised.

He shrugged. "It was my sister's favorite comfort food so I figured I would cover all the bases. I didn't know what you had in the house, so I got stuff to make breakfast too."

Mason pulled out eggs, pancake mix, and orange juice. He was only in the store for ten minutes. She couldn't imagine what else he would have gotten if he had more time.

"You are like Mary Poppins. You aren't going to pull a talking parrot umbrella out of there are you?"

# Three

"Mary, breakfast is done." Mason put the plate piled high with pancakes on the table. "Do you think we should try waking Mia up?"

They glanced into their patient's room. She was tucked into the center of the bed with her mouth wide open.

Mary pulled out a kitchen chair and sat down. "I checked on her a bit ago and she had drool running down her chin. She took a pain pill almost two hours ago, so she is going to be out for a while."

"I'm concerned they are overmedicating her. She's so tiny and the medicine seems to really knock her out." Mason bit his lip as he stared at his plate.

Mary squinted her eyes as she thought for a second, "Lacey's a nurse, isn't she? Maybe after class, you can bring her by?"

Relief flooded Mason's face. "I completely forgot what she does. That's a brilliant idea."

Mary beamed at him.

"Are you sure you're okay missing class and staying with her?" he asked.

Mary sat forward. "I'm happy to stay here. She's going to need help and I didn't have any plans today."

"Thanks, I'll open the gym, teach our regular class, then head back here. I'll see if Lacey has time to stop by with me." He glanced back in at Mia and forced himself to swallow his guilt.

*** 

"Great class ladies, as always you showed how strong you are and I'm proud of how far you've all come." Mason clapped along with the class.

He looked around the room. There were eight of them, plus Mary, who attended religiously.

They came from different walks of life, were different ages, and all had a story. Some had been abused, others suffered loss, and some were unwanted, but they found solace in this class, and that was exactly why he'd started it two years ago.

One of the girls from the back of the room waved him down, "Mason, where's Mary? I don't think she's ever missed a class." Melissa chewed her bottom lip anxiously.

Mason looked around the room and was glad to see everyone seemed to share her question. He was excited to see they were bonding, even if it was only here at the gym.

"Actually, I stopped a girl from getting attacked last night. She is alone and needed someone to stay with her after we left the emergency room. I asked Mary if she would keep her company so that Mia, the girl, would feel more comfortable." He glanced over at Lacey. "I am heading back over there. I thought maybe if you had time, you could come with me? I think she's taking too high a dose of pain meds."

"Of course, I can follow you over there." Lacey rushed to get her bag.

"Thank God you were there." Maria made the sign of the cross. He smiled, but inside he cringed. God had nothing to do with it. How could there be a God that let so many bad things happen to good people? He had lost his religion long ago, but respected everyone's choice to believe what they wanted to. Given everything these women had been through, he found it amazing any of them still had their faith.

He fist-bumped or high fived each woman as they left the room. Lacey stood by the door waiting for him. He shut off the lights to the classroom and waved goodbye to his staff as he walked through the gym and left.

Lacey followed behind in her car as he drove back to Mia's. He was pleasantly surprised to see Mary and Mia sitting on the porch swing.

She looked a lot better than she had when he'd left earlier.

Mason waved as he walked up. "I see our patient is up and about, did you eat breakfast?" He looked between the two of them.

Mia smiled and nodded at the woman next to him. "Mary has been great. I did eat some eggs and I'm feeling a lot less queasy now."

Mason pointed toward Lacey to introduce her, "This is Lacey, she goes to the same gym classes as Mary, and happens to be a nurse. I asked her to come check up on you."

Heat rushed Mia's cheeks, "I'm a little embarrassed by all this attention. I hate to take you away from your lives."

Mason, Lacey, and Mary all gave her the same exasperated look.

"I know you aren't from the South, so I'll forgive your lack of knowledge, but honey, we take care of our own around here. If Mason asks for help, then we'll be here to give it." Lacey smiled sweetly at Mia before walking closer and holding her hand out. "May I take a look?"

Mia held her arm up but didn't say a word. Lacey gently pulled back the bandage and peaked at the incision. "The doctor did a great job, I'd be shocked if you have much of a scar." She carefully resealed the bandage. "I know Mason was worried the painkillers were too strong for you, if you are struggling to stay awake and are having trouble speaking coherently, you probably don't need so much in your system. Over the next two days you should try to last longer between doses. You can even start alternating with Advil or Tylenol. If you'd like, I can stop by tomorrow and help you clean it and change the bandages?"

Tears welled in Mia's eyes.

Lacey grabbed her hand and squeezed gently. "If you are still in pain don't wait, take the medication."

"It's not that. I still can't believe how nice all of you are being. Maybe if I tell my parents about all the help you guys have been offering, they will stop insisting they come out and take care of me."

Mason leaned against the rail of the porch. "If you want me to talk to your dad again, I'm happy to."

Mia smiled. "I talked to him this morning. You made quite the impression on him last night."

Mary chuckled at their embarrassment. "You did. I heard him asking her all kinds of questions about you."

"I bet all dads would love him, he's our knight in shining armor." Lacey teased.

Mason held his hands up. "I never claimed to be a parent whisperer, but I'm willing to help in any way I can. Now, I say we go inside and put on a movie. Lacey, you are welcome to join us if you'd like?"

Lacey glanced at Mia, "That's up to Mia. If you don't mind my sweaty, hot mess on your couch, I can stay around for a bit."

It occurred to Mason that Lacey may be as lonely as the rest of them were. She was divorced and didn't have kids so she may have been as glad to make new friends as Mia and Mary were.

"Absolutely, the more the merrier." Mia waved her to follow them inside.

As for Mason, he struggled to admit to himself that Mia had gotten under his skin. He realized he was attracted to her even though she was the opposite of every girl he had ever dated. He was intrigued by her, and was happy to help. He wanted to get to know her if she was willing to let him.

The real question was whether Mia wanted to get to know him.

# Four

Monday morning Mia laid in bed staring up at the ceiling. She hadn't realized how isolated she had become living in a place where she knew no one. Even though the circumstances surrounding how she met her new friends weren't the greatest, she had to admit this was the best weekend she'd had since moving to Savannah.

Between Mason, Lacey, and Mary, she never had a moment alone, which was probably good. She knew if she had quiet time, she would likely start thinking about the attack again. Distractions were definitely the best tactic.

Lacey and Mary had gone on and on about their defense class. She was intrigued, and willing to step foot in the gym, even though she swore she never would again. Mia knew there was a backstory that Mason wasn't telling her, and the mystery of it all was driving her insane. She was always too curious for her own good.

Mia knew her boss at the library was unhappy about her returning to work but after a little persuasion he agreed. He had urged her to take time off but she knew if she sat at home while everyone else was at work, she would be miserable, staring at the clock all day.

Some people would think working at a library would be boring but not Mia. She knew she could turn down any aisle, pick up any book, and be transported to another time or place. She loved talking to reluctant readers and helping them pick out a book that they could fall in love with. It could hardly be called work because she didn't dread it like most people did.

At five forty-five she shut off her computer and walked the few blocks over to the gym. As she made her way through the streets she realized she often walked around in her own world. She had to stop doing that because she promised herself she wouldn't be an easy target ever again. Her naivety was gone and in its place was a bit of anxiety and shaky hands.

As the red brick building came into view, butterflies danced in her belly. She peeked inside the large picture window and saw two men covered in sweat, sparring in a large boxing ring in the center of the room. The butterflies turned to rampaging elephants. She had not expected a bunch of macho guys beating on each other to be the first thing she saw.

Mia didn't think twice. She spun on her heels and tried to get away quickly, coming face to face with Mary.

She squealed, "You came! I can't wait for you to meet the rest of the girls." Mary was oblivious to the dread churning in Mia's gut. She grabbed Mia and dragged her into the gym with her.

Once inside Mia was surprised to see the gym was much bigger than the boxing ring suggested. Exercise machines were spread along all four walls. Men and women of various ages worked out alongside each other. The women didn't appear intimidated in the least, she took that as a good sign.

Mary still had a tight grip on Mia's good hand and she pulled her along to a door in the back of the gym that led to another room with mirrors running along the back wall. Several women were standing around stretching. Mason was in the corner messing with a stereo.

Seeing him in his workout clothes made her mouth go dry. She never had any appreciation for muscly guys, but something about him made heat rush through her body.

Arms wrapped around Mia from behind. She glanced over her shoulder to see Lacey with a huge smile on her face. "I'm so glad you're here."

"Okay ladies, let's fight those demons of ours." Loud music blasted through the speakers.

Mason spun around, he did a double take when he saw Mia against the back wall. He smiled and nodded to her. She smiled then turned to sit on the bench in the corner.

For the next forty-five minutes they worked so hard that steam fogged up most of the mirrors. When Mason said to fight their demons, she thought he really meant punish them. Beads of sweat rolled down their faces as each woman pushed herself harder. It didn't matter their size or age, they gave everything they had, and Mason was masterful at encouraging them to keep giving more.

After their cooldown, each woman walked up to the mirrors and stopped a foot away. Mason and the nine women stood in a line staring at themselves in the mirror. Mia had no clue what was happening.

"Time to speak your truth, I'll start with mine." Mason cleared his throat, glanced at Mia in the mirror, and then focused back on himself again. "I forgive myself."

They were such small words yet Mia felt each one like a knife in her gut. She could see the hatred and anger flash in his eyes momentarily. Before she could contemplate further, the rest of the group went.

A young Hispanic woman at the end of the line said, "I am not what happened to me."

Next to her was a girl that didn't even look old enough to drive. Mia was scared to hear her truth. What demon was she fighting at such a young age?

"There is nothing wrong with me." Even though she was staring at herself confidently, the words were whispered, as if she didn't believe them. The girl glanced at Mason in the mirror and shrugged apologetically.

He smiled and nodded.

Lacey was next in line; her voice was strong. "I am *not* what happened to me." Mia was surprised by the force she put on the word "not".

Mia's stomach was starting to turn. She still had to get through six more declarations. Her heart was breaking for these strangers.

A beautiful blonde a little older than Mia pushed her glasses further up her nose and straightened her shoulders before speaking. "I deserve to have my needs met." She nodded at herself in the mirror.

Next to her was a tough looking girl with short, spiky, black hair. Power was radiating off of her. If anyone in the class had a chance of beating their demons, it was this girl. "I AM NOT WHAT HAPPENED TO ME." The girl roared in the mirror. No one else in the room flinched, obviously, anger was normal for her. She turned to the short, chubby lady next to her and nodded encouragement.

The middle-aged woman stared down at her feet for a second before peaking up. "I am strong enough to leave."

Mia's heart lurched. Even she could hear the woman didn't believe the words she was saying. She wasn't sure she could take much more but three more women still had to go.

A girl around Mia's age was next. Standing behind her, she could see scars along the girl's arms. Her fists were balled at her side as she stared at herself in the mirror. "I am not what happened to me." Mia was starting to see a lot of them shared the same mantra.

The woman next to her was biting her lip nervously.

Mason nodded encouragingly to the woman. "You got this Kayla."

"To escape fear, I have to go through it, not around it." She let out a deep breath, as if the words had been strangling her. Then she smiled shyly at Mason.

Last up was Mary. Mia was scared to hear what she would say. Mary glanced at Mia briefly before looking back in the mirror. "My life matters."

Mia felt something cold on her hand. She looked down and realized it was a teardrop. Desperate for these women to not see her crying, she stared up at the ceiling trying to get control. She didn't want any of them to think she was pitying them. That wasn't what they needed.

Mason glanced at Mia in the mirror briefly. "Excellent job, ladies. Remember, it's not enough to say the words, we have to live them too. I'll see you guys Wednesday."

Mia loved how close the group seemed as each woman took turns either hugging or high fiving Mason before collecting their stuff. As they left, they nodded and smiled at Mia.

The tough-looking girl walked up to Mia and held her hand out. "Hi, I'm Andy, and I'm guessing you are Mia, Mason's latest rescue."

Mia wasn't sure if she should be offended. She was making her sound like a stray animal.

"I'm sorry, that probably sounded rude, most of us were rescued in some way by Mason." She glanced down at Mia's bandaged arm. "I hope when you are feeling better, you'll join us." She smiled and left the room.

Mia found Mason standing by the mirrors talking to the young Hispanic girl. More than ever, she was desperate to know him. It was obvious he was something special and Mia's heart was screaming at her to take a chance on him, while her brain was questioning if she was even in his league.

Now she had to decide if she was brave enough to go after him.

# Five

"Mia, I'm so glad you made it. What did you think?" Mason grabbed a towel and wiped his face.

Mia had never found sweat sexy before but suddenly she was enjoying watching the small beads of liquid roll down the muscles of Mason's arms.

"I don't think I've ever seen a workout class like that before, it was intense in a lot of ways." Mia couldn't get the words each woman said out of her head.

"I don't think any of us think of it as exercise. It's more like therapy with a touch of aggression." Mary joked as she wiped the sweat from her face and tucked her towel in her gym bag. She elbowed Mia in the side, "We almost lost her though, she got one look at the guys boxing out front and was ready to head for the hills."

Mia gave Mary the side eye for ratting her out.

Mason frowned. "I didn't think of that. I should have warned you since you did mention you don't like gyms with macho guys."

Mia blushed at him bringing up what she said while she was high on pain meds in the hospital.

"They're actually big babies. You'll have to come by sometime and watch when Andy gets in the ring with them. She's like a spastic spider monkey and kicks their asses." He smiled like a proud papa.

Mia stepped back as Mason reached around her to open the classroom door. "She definitely seemed like she could take care of herself." Goosebumps ran down Mia's body as the cold air from the main part of the gym hit them.

"She didn't start that way. When she first came here she couldn't even go the whole class without having to take a break. Lucky for her she had so much anger from her situation, it fueled her to become the warrior you met today." Mason waited for the girls to walk out first.

Mia contemplated his words. She never had a desire to workout but her perspective had changed in the last week. She knew if she were attacked again, she wasn't any better prepared to handle it herself.

The threesome stood awkwardly for a minute before Mary finally spoke up. "Well, I guess I'll be going. If you need anything you have my cell phone number." She wrapped Mia in a tight hug and whispered in her ear, "Go get him, girl." She leaned back, winked at her, and left the gym.

Mary's words echoed in her mind. She needed a distraction or her nerves would go into full panic mode. "So, everyone in there is a victim?"

She regretted immediately saying it like that, but after all their declarations, it seemed the best word she could think of.

"I don't like that word and I don't think they do either. Some of them consider themselves survivors, and the others, fighters. Not everyone has pushed past their demons, but hopefully each week they get a little closer." Mason didn't look at her as he walked the rest of the gym, nodding at or fist bumping his clients. It was obvious he was well-liked and took his job seriously.

"Who are you?" Mia winced as soon as the words came out of her mouth. Heat rushed her face. "I'm sorry, I just mean, you can't be much older than me, yet you're this saint that goes around rescuing people and helping them heal. You seem so together."

The muscle in Mason's jaw ticked. He didn't seem to like something she said. "I promise you I'm no saint. I'm definitely no one special." He grabbed a discarded towel off the floor and walked to the nearest basket. "How about you have dinner with me tonight and I'll tell you my story?"

Mia bit her lip trying to look calm on the outside while inside she was dancing a jig. "Are you sure? I know I've taken a lot of your time the last few days." She held her breath, hoping he would disagree. She wanted to spend more time with him and desperately wanted to know his background.

"There is nowhere else I'd rather be, but I do need to shower first. Do you mind waiting while I run into the locker room? You can sit in my office while you wait."

Mia saw genuine interest in his eyes. She was still struggling to accept that this beautiful man wanted to spend time with her.

"I can wait. I have a book in my purse, so I likely won't even notice how long you are gone." She shrugged unapologetically.

"Alright, we have a date. Follow me." Mason missed the slight bulge of Mia's eyes at his words. He spun around and led her to the back.

His office was small and nothing extravagant. He had letters and note cards pinned up on the walls, and pictures of him with happy clients mixed throughout. "Make yourself comfortable, I'll be back in a flash."

Mia knew there was a book begging to be read, but the letters on the wall interested her more. If she didn't think he was a saint before she did now. Every note was from a client who owed their success to him. It wasn't just women he rescued writing to him, large muscular men thanked him too.

Mia gently stroked the bandage on her arm as she read story after story. It felt like only five minutes had passed when Mason came strolling in.

Her mouth went instantly dry as she took in his just showered look. She resisted reaching up and running her hands through his still damp hair. It was his fault; his cologne was intoxicating.

"All set?" He grabbed his keys and cell phone off his desk and held the office door open for her. She walked quietly beside him as they left the gym. She could feel curious stares on them. They likely assumed she was a potential customer earlier, but now that he was leaving with her, people seemed more interested in her.

He held the door to the gym open for her. "If you're up for Italian there's a place a couple of doors down."

"Pasta is always good with me." She said a silent prayer, hoping the food wouldn't be good. She had a weakness for garlic bread and pasta, and didn't want to stuff herself in front of him.

They quietly walked the short distance to the restaurant and smiled shyly at each other as they waited to be taken to a table. Unsure what to say, Mia looked around instead. The walls were painted to look like large blocks, vines and grapes hung around the room. Outdoor light posts and benches were spread around making it feel like you were at an outdoor café.

It didn't take long for the hostess to seat them. She perused the menu quickly and went with the same thing she always ordered at Italian restaurants, chicken parmigiana.

Once their order was in and the bread and oil were in front of them, they had nothing left to distract them.

Mason spoke first, "I can feel the curiosity emanating from you. I'm good with telling you my history but I'll warn you now it isn't pretty, this is your last chance, you can still turn back." Mason winked to lessen the ominous tone to his words.

# Six

"I'm sorry, you are such an enigma, I can't figure you out and it's making me crazy." Mia dunked a piece of bread in the oil and chewed quietly, waiting for him to answer.

He glanced around the restaurant. They were in a near-empty section and the lights were dim. He shrugged and started his tale. "I had the perfect childhood, my parents loved my sister and me, we were given everything we could ever want. I was your typical jock in high school. I played football and soccer, so I was always with the guys either working out or practicing."

His hand shook slightly as he picked up his water and took a large gulp. "My sister and I grew apart. She was the bookworm and I was the partier. My senior year I noticed she had become more withdrawn than normal, but I was too selfish to care."

His voice hitched on the last word. "One day I was running late to practice and I saw her hiding in the stairwell at school crying. You know what I did?" Mason's knuckles were white from the fist he was making. "Absolutely nothing. I kept walking. Right past her."

Mia's heart hurt for him. "You don't have to finish, we can talk about something else." She practically begged him to tell her his past, and now she was wishing she could close Pandora's box.

"I have to face my past, I can't do that if I am ignoring it." He took a deep breath. "That was the last time I saw my sister alive. My parents found her the next morning. She had swallowed pretty much every prescription drug we had in the house."

Mia didn't mean to cry, but after watching the tears fall silently down his cheeks she couldn't help herself. She sat back and let him take his time processing his memories.

"It took a while, but we found out one of her teachers had attacked her and had continued to assault her for months after. He saw an introverted, shy kid and took advantage of her. And here's the best part, that fucker never spent a day in jail." His fist slammed down onto the table causing the silverware to clink together. "We went to a very expensive private school. They fired the teacher and gave my parents a huge settlement if they agreed to keep it quiet."

Mason leaned forward, rage burning in his eyes. "I begged my parents not to take the deal. I wanted the whole school to burn to the ground but my parents were more worried about appearances, so they took the money. I think that hurt worse than losing her. It felt like she was being victimized all over again."

Mason shrugged, for a second, he stared at the table, lost in his own thoughts. "Nothing was the same after that. I quit sports and stopped going to school. They weren't stupid.

They gave me my diploma anyways. The day I turned eighteen I demanded my parents give me the money so I could do something good with it. I think they knew they screwed up because they didn't fight me on it. I used it to open the gym and named it after her. I want it to be a haven for other people to feel they have a safe place to go because my sister...Raven didn't."

Mason fiddled with his silverware before continuing on, his voice shook as he forced the words out. "And now you know why I spend every day fighting...I'm fighting to forgive myself for not being there for her. I will never turn my back on a person in need again." He used both hands to wipe the tears from his face, then leaned back and took a few deep breaths. "I'm sorry, it's always difficult to talk about."

Even though Mia barely knew him, she found herself getting up and walking around the table. She kneeled on the bench next to him and wrapped her arms around him. There were no sexual overtones, no ulterior motives. She just wanted to comfort him like his parents obviously never had. He didn't resist, he melted against her and wrapped his arms around her.

Over his shoulder the waitress caught her eye. She was obviously conflicted about interrupting them during their intense moment. Mia held her finger up, silently asking her to give them another minute. They sat like that for a little longer, till he finally let go and sat back.

"I'm so sorry, I'm usually more controlled." He glanced around the room, embarrassment obvious on his face.

"What you've gone through, and how you've overcome it, is a miracle. You're doing a wonderful thing. I read the letters from people at the gym. Your sister would be proud of what you have accomplished in her name."

"The crazy thing is, I actually do feel a little better. Normally it takes me hours if not days to fully pull out of the misery that overwhelms me after talking about her. Maybe you helped me banish one of those demons haunting me."

Before Mia could respond, the waitress returned with their meals. With a new level of intimacy between them, they ate in comfortable silence.

## Seven

After dinner, Mason wouldn't let Mia take any form of public transportation home. She thought it was sweet he worried about her safety. She was never going to admit to him that she wasn't thrilled with the idea either. Originally, she was going to Uber home as soon as the class was over, but that was early evening when the sun was still out. She hadn't gone out in the dark since the attack. Maybe after a few of his classes, she would be ready.

"You know it occurred to me how much fun Mary and Lacey have been having hanging out with you. I was thinking maybe the rest of the group might like meeting up outside of class." Mason stood in front of Mia on her porch.

"My house is big enough, I don't mind hosting here if you want?" She tried not to look too eager, but the idea of new friends was exciting. She knew she was lonely before, but it wasn't till the last few days she realized just how isolated she had become. She loved her books, but this was the first time in her life she realized she needed human interaction too.

Mason fiddled with the keys in his hand. "Are you sure? That's a lot to ask when you don't even know these women."

"I'm absolutely sure, I can do any night this week. Or we can wait for the weekend."

"I'll text the group and see what works, but I'm buying the food and drinks, deal?" He held his hand out, waiting for her to shake on it.

She hesitantly held her hand out and shook. Neither moved, their hands clasped, looking into each other's eyes.

Eventually, Mason broke contact first. He took a deep breath and slowly slid his hand from hers. "I'll let you know as soon as I hear from everyone." He leaned forward. She moved to meet him halfway. He smiled then turned and left.

She was mortified, she had thought he was going to kiss her.

"Don't be daft, Mia." She muttered to herself before going inside and curling up with a book.

After the third time reading the same page, she tossed the book to the side. She had tried to focus on the pages in front of her, but the excitement and nervousness of the party had her panicking. It felt like high school all over again. What if they didn't like her?

# Eight

Mason sat in his car with his head resting on the steering wheel. In the six years since his sister died, this was the first time he felt desire again for a woman. The year after her death he was completely shut off from the world, wallowing in grief.

One day sitting in the lobby of his grief counselor's office waiting for his appointment, a news segment on television caught his attention. It was a girl a little older than him. She had been attacked by a family member when she was younger. The attack drove her to train in multiple forms of martial arts and self-defense so she would never be a victim again.

Her first year in college she was leaving the library late and heard a muffled cry in the bushes. A young girl was being held down by a man on top of her. She told the newscaster that she didn't even hesitate. Her training kicked in and she fought off the attacker. She never considered her preparation might save another person.

That story changed his life, saved him from the dark path he had been walking. After Raven's death, he had lost his religion, because in his mind, if there was a God, he wouldn't have allowed anything to happen to her. Desperate for a measure of sanity, he allowed himself to imagine she was in a better place free from the pain she had endured in her short life. He knew she must have died hating him and would never forgive him for not helping her, but maybe helping other women would be a step in the right direction.

A new fire burned in him from that day on. He took Raven's blood money and dedicated his life to helping people. Unfortunately, in the few years he'd ran the gym, he met way more victims, both men and women, than he ever expected and it changed him.

He wasn't sure how to be intimate again, he had a new view on what women went through and was scared to cause someone to be uncomfortable from his advances.

So, that night, standing in front of Mia, he was flustered. On the one hand, he wanted to kiss her, while on the other, he was terrified to try. It didn't take long for his brain to stop him. His heart had started racing, he panicked, and left.

Tomorrow was a new day, maybe he would be ready to take a chance on love again. Letting out a growl of frustration, he sat up and grabbed his phone. One by one, he called each woman in his class and invited them over for dinner. He was surprised and pleased when almost all of them said they could meet up the next evening. Now he wouldn't have to come up with an excuse to see her again.

His stomach did somersaults as he dialed Mia. He glanced towards her house, hoping to see a light come on or catch her passing by a window. After a few rings, it went to voicemail. His stomach dropped because he knew she was inside and had ignored his call. Trained to not make someone uncomfortable, he hung up without leaving a voicemail.

He tossed the phone into the passenger seat and drove home. As he pulled into the parking lot of his apartment complex, his phone lit up. It was Mia. She was calling him back.

He cleared his throat, and tried to sound calm. "Hello?"

"Hey, it's Mia, sorry I missed your call. I was in the shower. It takes a lot longer when I can only use one arm."

He pumped his fist in the air, she hadn't been ignoring him. "Oh, I didn't mean to bother you. I wanted to let you know I talked to the group and they are good with dinner tomorrow night, if that still works for you?"

"Wow, that was fast."

"I can move it to later if you want. I should have thought about waiting till your arm was better." He ran his hand through his hair, feeling like an idiot.

"I probably shouldn't admit this and sound like a loser, but I have absolutely nothing going on tomorrow, so I would be happy to have everyone over." She chuckled softly.

"Awesome, I told them six-thirty. Is it okay if I come over at six to put out the food and drinks?"

"Six is good for me. Do you want me to pick anything up?"

"No, this was my idea, plus you are providing the location, so that is plenty." He knew the conversation was winding down and he couldn't think of another reason to keep her on the phone.

"Okay, then I'll see you tomorrow."

"Sounds good, have a good night." Mason rolled his eyes, that sounded lame.

"You too, bye." Mia hung up.

In high school he had been a lot smoother. He was seriously out of practice.

# Nine

Mia's alarm went off like normal Tuesday morning. She grabbed her phone and dialed her boss. "Hi Sam, it's Mia. You were right, it was a little early for me to come back to work. If it's okay I'm going to take off today and try again tomorrow." She felt bad about the lie but if she was having people over, she wanted to do a deep cleaning of every nook and cranny in the house.

"Of course, take your time, let's keep tomorrow tentative, too. Call me if you decide not to come in."

"Thank you and sorry for the short notice."

She tossed her phone on the bed and rushed around to get dressed. Even though she had been here six months, she hadn't done much to make it cozy. She needed to run to the store and buy supplies.

With her shopping list running through her head, she grabbed her purse and headed for the door. She made it onto the porch before realizing her car was still impounded. "Well, shit."

For a brief second, she thought about calling Mason or one of her other new friends, but decided against it. She didn't want to explain why she was buying home decor items when she had been living there for months.

Uber was turning into her best friend. She requested a car and sat on the porch until it arrived, then had him drop her at Target. The best part about having the day off was that she was able to take her time deciding what she wanted.

She felt so grown up as she walked the aisles trying to decide what her style was. She decided she liked the contrast between reds, blacks, and whites. She also had a fondness for roses so she did a happy dance when she found a couple of paintings that matched her new theme. Her house was going to look like a home for the first time since she moved in. It filled her with an unexpected sense of pride.

As she passed the aisles of dishes it dawned on her she had nothing for entertaining. They probably wouldn't judge her for her mismatch of plastic and glass cups but she didn't have anything that resembled a wine glass. She grabbed a set for white wine and a set for red. For good measure she grabbed beer glasses and a few platters.

Glancing down at her overflowing cart she laughed at herself, "I guess I'm officially an adult now."

She checked out and ordered another Uber. She bounced on her toes as she waited excitedly for her ride so she could get home and get ready for her party.

# Ten

Thirty minutes before the rest of the group was due to arrive Mason rang Mia's doorbell. His arms were weighed down by grocery bags, and he wanted to look strong and tough, but if she didn't hurry, he was going to have to put something down. "Why did I have to try to get all the groceries on one try?" Mason rolled his eyes, "Oh, because I like her and now I have to show off." He mumbled to himself.

As his arms were starting to ache, the door swung open. Her yellow dress matched her hair and made him think of sunshine. "I love that you are punctual, let me help you with those." She reached forward to help.

"I'm a delicately balanced mess. If one thing moves, I might lose all of it."

"You better get in here and put that stuff down then." She stepped back and held the door wide for him.

As he walked, he noticed small changes from the last time he was there. She'd added flowers, candles, and pictures to the wall.

He suddenly felt trapped.

Did he compliment how nice it looked because she obviously worked hard? Or did he pretend not to notice in case she would be embarrassed by him pointing it out? Sometimes it sucked being a guy.

He set the bags down on the kitchen island. "I like the flowers." He mentally patted himself on the back for the nonchalant comment.

"Thanks." She smiled shyly at him. "So, what did you bring?"

Mason pulled out multiple bottles of wine, a case of beer, a bottle of Sprite, and a Coke. "I thought we could make it casual so people can take what they want." The groceries didn't stop, he handed her deli meats and cheeses, "Do you want to put these on a plate and I'll cut up the tomato and lettuce?"

"Wow, you've thought of everything." She glanced at the bag containing a large bowl of fruit salad.

"I take my sandwiches very seriously, building the perfect sammy is a work of art." He winked before opening the fridge and putting the drinks away.

After the blundered kiss the night before, nerves had him rushing around like he was on speed. At least tonight there would be more people with them to help distract him from obsessing over both the desire to kiss her, and the need to make up for leaving her hanging the night before.

Over the next few hours he needed to impress her if he wanted any hope of her dating him.

## *Eleven*

Mia took one last glance around the kitchen and living room. Everything was in place and ready for her first get-together at her house.

At exactly six-thirty, the doorbell rang. She had a feeling she knew who would be the first to arrive. Mason walked with her to the door. Just as she expected, "Hi Mary, come on in."

"Thanks, I made brownies." She placed a large plate into Mason's waiting hands.

As Mia was about to close the door, she noticed her next guests walking up the sidewalk. Mason waited until they were at the door before doing introductions. "Mia, this is Maria and Allison."

"Nice to officially meet you both." She stood back and waved them to come inside.

"Hi girls, come on back, I'll get you a drink." Mary waved to the other women to join her in the kitchen, leaving Mia and Mason to stay by the door to greet more people.

"Here comes the youngest of the group." Mason pointed as the teenager from the class got out of a car, quickly followed by the tough looking girl that Mia remembered thinking didn't need help with self-defense.

"Ladies, glad you could make it. Tonya, I know it's a school night so we won't keep you all night." Mason smiled apologetically at Tonya.

"My parents are out of town anyways; my brother is picking me up later." She glanced over to Mia. "Thank you for inviting us." She passed by and waved to the growing group of women hanging out in the kitchen.

Mia smiled as she listened to the sounds echoing around the house. She didn't realize how much she'd missed being with other people.

"Andy, it's nice to see you again." Mia held her hand out to the tough looking girl. "I heard you can take down any guy at the gym." She hoped flattery would help win her a friend.

Andy beamed. "I do my best to put them in their place, this guy though-" she playfully punched Mason's shoulder "won't fight me. I think he's afraid to lose face when I take him down."

"I'm waiting till you're ready, I don't want to knock you down too fast. Maybe one day you'll be ready for me." Mason mocked her as she walked by.

"Hey, someone I know." Mia gave Lacey a hug as she walked in the house.

"Sorry I'm late, we had three ambulances pull up as soon as I was about to clock out, so I stayed to help." The lines around Lacey's eyes showed how tired she was.

"You're not late at all. Everyone's in the back grabbing a drink." Mason high-fived her as she walked by.

One last person strolled up the walkway to the porch. "Last but not least, Melissa." Mason ushered her in before closing the door.

Mia waved and smiled at the girl. From across the classroom she had thought the girl looked tortured, up close she could see there were definitely demons haunting her eyes. Mia was almost afraid to find out what gave this young girl such haunted looks.

"Ready for this?" Mason stood in front of Mia, giving her a second to collect herself before going into the room full of women who already knew each other.

"Shouldn't there be two more?" Mia asked.

"This is it for tonight." He waved his arm to let her go first.

As they entered the living room, everyone turned to look at them. "There's plenty of food, at least until I make a plate so you better dig in." Mason jokingly pushed through the crowd to be first in line.

Mia chatted with Mary as the rest of the group made plates and settled in around the room.

"Mason, where are Jane and Kayla?" Andy asked as she sat next to Tonya on the couch.

"They both declined." Mia could tell Mason was trying not to go into detail.

"I was really starting to think you were getting somewhere with those two." Tonya glanced at Mia. "Jane has an asshole for a husband, he abuses her and runs her life. I'm sure he wouldn't let her come. Then there's Kayla, she has that thing where it she can't leave the house or she panics, what's it called?" She glanced over to Lacey.

"She has agoraphobia." Lacey answered.

"That's right, it was so bad she missed her grandmother's funeral. After that, she started going to therapy and then our class. As far as I know, those are the only two places she goes outside of the house." She bit into her sandwich and shook her head in irritation, as if the two missing women were there to see her disappointment.

Mia chewed her pasta salad as she thought about the women around her. They all seemed so happy despite having horrible things happen to them.

Andy cleared her throat to get everyone's attention. "My story. I grew up in a podunk town outside of Birmingham that was full of religious zealots. One day I was walking home from school and a group of guys jumped me and tried to beat the gay out of me. My family looked the other way rather than acknowledge what happened, because then they would have to face why it happened." Andy took a gulp from the beer she was holding. "The day I turned eighteen I took off and haven't looked back."

"I'm so sorry that happened to you. Everyone deserves their families unconditional support." Mia's heart ached for the girl. From all outward appearances she was tough, but after a closer look, she could see the vulnerability Andy tried to hide.

Mia turned at the scoffing noises both Melissa and Allison made. Allison leaned forward, "I think it's more unusual to have a supportive family than not." Subconsciously she twisted her napkin in her hands. "My dad beat my mom my entire life. I begged her to leave him, but she refused. When I was eighteen, I was done begging, and I left." She stared down at her lap for a few seconds, lost in some memory. "I hear from her sometimes, but not much has changed. My boyfriend Jack says it's for the best, so I don't try to see her anymore."

Mia thought her statement about Jack sounded odd, but who was she to judge.

Melissa cleared her throat to get the group's attention. "If we're giving our sob stories, I guess I'll go next." She cleared her throat, rolled her neck from side to side and sat straight as if she was preparing for a fight. "My brother was mentally ill for as far back as I can remember. My parents thought it was just him acting out. They didn't want to admit he had a real problem. When I was thirteen, I woke up to screaming. Billy came rushing into my room with a knife and attacked me. After a minute of struggling...sorry this is always tough to talk about. I managed to slip around him and run to the neighbors for help."

Mia was horrified as she watched Melissa rubbing her arms absently. Faint scars ran along the skin. "My parents didn't make it." Her voice hitched, she was barely controlling her despair. "My brother is locked away and I wake up every day thinking about how I'm the only one who survived." She glanced around at the group before looking back at Mia. "I've considered going to see him. Logically I know he's ill, but then I think about my mom and dad and part of me wants to see him suffer."

Lacey leaned over and squeezed Melissa's shoulder before looking at Mia. "No one did anything to me, I did it to myself. Despite my best efforts I was never able to carry a baby full term. I've had a few miscarriages." Lacey's hand was resting on her stomach as if there were still a baby there. "The stress of it all drove a wedge between my husband and I and we divorced. The loss of both the children we almost had and my marriage left me feeling helpless and not in control of my own life. I use these classes to help me feel strong again." She glanced around and shrugged. "I have bad days like anyone but for the most part I feel a little less guilty, a little less like it was all my fault."

Melissa slammed her glass down on the side table. "You have nothing to feel guilty about and your ex is an asshole if he ever blamed you."

Murmurs of agreement echoed around the room. Lacey laughed as she wiped a tear from her cheek.

"I guess I'm one of the lucky ones." Tonya glanced around shyly. "My family is very supportive, but they want me to be safe. I get bullied in school and they're afraid it's going to escalate. I will say it has gotten better since I started coming here. I don't know if I look different or am acting different, but I don't get messed with quite as much as I used to."

Andy nudged Tonya's knee, "I remember the first day you came in. I thought a strong wind was going to knock you over. I told Mason he was crazy for letting you into the class. I was afraid we were going to hurt you." Andy leaned towards Tonya. "Now you are fierce looking."

Mia thought the blush that spread across both girl's cheeks was sweet.

Maria got up and went to the kitchen catching everyone's attention. She was the only one who hadn't shared yet, and Mia had a feeling she wasn't going to.

Mary leaned over and whispered to Mia, "Bad college experience." Mia had a feeling she knew what that meant, and she felt for the girl.

Lacey smiled warmly at the women around the room before ending on Mia, "As you can tell, we are all in the class for different reasons. Hopefully you'll join us when your arm is better?"

"Thank you all for being brave enough to share your stories. I know it was difficult for you. I'm still thinking about joining but you've definitely helped me see the bigger picture, that it isn't just a class."

Mason set his plate on the coffee table. "I echo what Mia said. I've known a little about each of you but now I know what each of you are facing and hopefully I can come up with ways to help each of you." He turned and looked at Mia. "The gym is always open if you decide to join us. No pressure though, and enough serious talk. Let's get dessert." Mason jumped up and made a beeline for the makeshift buffet.

Mia gave him credit, he was in a room full of women giving their sob stories and he gave strength when it was warranted and lightened the mood when it was needed.

She sat back and studied the people around her. Somehow, she had managed to find some of the bravest, and sweetest people she had ever met. She couldn't contain her smile knowing she was lucky enough to call them all friend.

# Twelve

Mason hadn't intended for the evening to turn into a therapy session but he felt that was the way it had been going. Maybe talking to people who had their own issues helped them, in which case who was he to stop them?

Eventually, the conversations shifted and everyone started discussing movies and music. It was good to see the group bonding over something fun for once.

"Well I hate to be the first to leave, but I have another long shift at the hospital tomorrow and I need to crash." Lacey stood and stretched. "Mia thank you for hosting. Mason, she told us this was your idea, so awesome job." She high fived him as she passed by on her way to the front door.

Lacey opened the door just as a guy was reaching up to ring the doorbell.

He jumped back as surprised at the door opening as she was to find someone standing there. "Oh hello, I'm here to pick up my sister Tonya?"

Tonya popped up. "Sorry I missed your texts." She reached over and hugged Mia. "Thanks again for having me over. I hope we see you in class."

"Hi, my name is Dallas," the newcomer extended his hand outward.

She reached out and shook the stranger's hand. "Hi, I'm Lacey."

Tonya walked up and linked arms with Lacey. "Can we walk her to her car, make sure she gets there safely?" She smiled sweetly at her big brother.

"Of course. Lead the way, ladies." The trio waved to the group as they closed the door behind them.

"Did you see the way Lacey was looking at him?" Mary giggled.

Mason shrugged. "I wasn't expecting him to be so much older than Tonya."

Maria glanced around the group. "Does anyone want the last brownie?"

"I'm good," Allison said. "I used to love brownies but now I like pound cake like Jack."

Mia stared at Allison like she had two heads. Mason noticed Allison always talked about herself and her boyfriend as if they were one person.

"I actually need to go. It's tough enough being perky for a room full of kindergarteners all day. It's even worse when I don't get enough sleep." Melissa grabbed her purse off the counter. "Mia, it was really nice getting to know you. I hope we see you in class."

It didn't take long before Mason was alone with Mia again. "Thank you again for letting us meet here. I think this was really good for the group."

"My house is open anytime. I had a lot of fun." Mia grabbed the empty dishes off the kitchen island and started loading the dishwasher.

"Let me do that. You don't need to try doing dishes with one arm." He rushed over and grabbed a bowl from her hand. "Go sit, I'll get this taken care of." He made a shooing gesture and turned back to the dishwasher.

Instead of taking his advice she stepped back and hopped up to sit on the kitchen counter rather than going out to the couch.

He grinned, "That can't be very comfortable."

"If you are going to do the hard work, the least I can do is stay here and entertain you." She crossed her ankles and leaned forward slightly. "Let's play a game, tell me something that grosses you out."

"Are you going to answer the questions too?"

"Absolutely, in fact, I'll go first." She pursed her lips, as if deep in thought. "Ass germs, has to be ass germs." She nodded matter-of-factly.

Mason nearly dropped the plate he was scraping clean above the garbage can. To say she shocked him would have been an understatement. He couldn't help but turn a questioning look towards her.

"What? The idea of people releasing gas from their asses that I must breathe in...it grosses me out. I mean think about it. If you hear someone fart, you know to hold your breath or run away. Unless they are the silent but deadly kind, you have no idea what you're inhaling until it's to late." She shook her head unapologetically, "It's the silent ones that get you."

If Mason wasn't already starting to fall for her he was now. He couldn't help the laughter that erupted from him. She was adorable and he itched to get closer to her.

"When you are done laughing at me, it's your turn to answer." Mia gave him a sardonic look.

"I don't think I can beat that. I mean, I was going to say earwax, but now it feels so boring."

"No, that works. Duly noted. There will be no kissing of ears."

Mason was thrown for a loop. She had been so reserved up to now. He liked this spunky side of her. He just didn't know what changed to bring it out.

"Okay, next question. What is your favorite smell?" Mia's legs swung back and forth as she waited for him to answer.

He dried his hands with a paper towel and leaned against the counter. "I am trying to come up with something not food related, but I'm struggling. I'll go with cinnamon rolls. One whiff and my mouth is watering."

"I get it, as far as food goes, I would say vanilla cake baking is mouthwatering for me." She pursed her lips and squinted her eyes, "This was a bad question. I am really full, but now I want cake and cinnamon rolls." Mia rubbed her belly as if she hadn't just stuffed herself at dinner.

"I'm sure we can make that happen if you want." He'd be willing to drive her all over town looking for open restaurants if it meant spending more time with her.

"If I eat any more tonight, I am definitely going to have to join your gym. Now for the million-dollar question," Mia cleared her throat, her breathing sped up, she was clearly nervous. "How long do I have to wait before you will kiss me?"

His mouth went dry. He knew that had to take a lot of courage. His stomach tightened, it was what he had wanted to do, and she was giving him the green light.

Mason balled up the paper towel and tossed it in the trash before walking over and stepping between her legs. They stared into each other's eyes. He could see the fear of rejection in her eyes, he hoped she could see the desire in his.

"That depends, how long will it take you to say Supercalifragilisticexpialidocious?"

"Supercal..."

Mason leaned in, wrapped his hand around the back of her neck, and pulled her lips to his. Goosebumps ran down his back. He hadn't realized how nervous he was until he'd finally done it. He would never admit it out loud but in high school, he kissed plenty of girls, and never got nervous. But this quiet bookworm had turned him inside out and made him a bundle of awkward nerves.

Minutes passed.

There was no longer a need for words.

Her soft lips tasted as good as he had expected. The fruity scent of her shampoo teased his senses. This moment would be seared in his memory forever.

As the desire inside him came close to boiling over, he pulled back. "I think-" he placed a kiss on her cheek. "I should-" he kissed the side of her neck. "Probably leave." He gently kissed her mouth one last time before pulling back. He was glad to see the slight glaze to her eyes. She was in the same state he was in. "Can I see you again this week?"

She nodded mutely, looking as if every bone in her body had melted.

"Call me tomorrow?" He squeezed her hand before stepping back.

"Will do." She hopped off the counter.

They held hands as she walked him to the door, "Lock up after I leave." He kissed her waiting mouth again. It was harder to step away. He needed to stop before he pushed things too far, too fast.

She gave him a mock salute. "Yes sir."

# Thirteen

Mia sat behind the checkout desk at the library daydreaming. The night before still didn't seem real. She had never been a very bold person, so asking Mason to kiss her shocked her as much as it did him. As soon as the words were out nausea had rushed through her, and the fear of rejection was a strong reminder of why she was a naturally shy person.

Her risk was rewarded though. She'd held her breath as he had sauntered up to her and stood between her legs. On the outside she probably looked calm. But on the inside, she felt like ants were crawling all over her.

Once he was in position, she froze up and had no idea what to do next.

Luckily, he did.

She'd been kissed before, but nothing compared to the feelings he had stirred inside her. It was the first time in her life she understood the passion she had read about for years. She loved romance books, but a small part of her always questioned if desire like that was real. Now she knew, and would never have such a naive outlook on love again.

Of course, it helped that she hadn't even made it to her bedroom before she got a goodnight text from him. The giddy feeling that surged through her made sleep impossible, so she did what she always did in her spare time, she baked.

Mia's attention was caught by her boss standing at the counter. "How'd you feel today, are you ready to come back full time, or do you need a few more days?" She was mortified he caught her staring off into space. "I don't want you overexerting yourself too soon."

She sat up and smoothed out her dress, trying to look more professional. "I feel a lot better. Thanks again for giving me yesterday off. I'll be back tomorrow, ready to go." She glanced at the clock and saw it was past five-thirty. Her thoughts of Mason had her leaving work late.

"If you're sure, I'll see you tomorrow." He smiled and walked away to help a kid that was clearly frustrated with the computer.

Mia packed up her belongings and hustled out the door. She was going to attend her first class at the gym, bandaged arm or not, it was happening.

She made it to Raven's Haven quickly and noticed that she was the first one there.

Mia smiled at the buff guy standing behind the counter. "Hello, I'd like to get a guest pass, I want to try out the six-thirty class." Only a couple of days with her new friends she was already more confident. She had no problem talking to the giant with bulging muscles.

He handed her a clipboard with two pages on it. "Absolutely, I just need you to fill out a couple of papers. Then you can go to the locker room to change."

She stood quietly, gave her information, and filled out the short survey about what her fitness goals were. It was harder than she expected because she really didn't have exercise goals. It was more a way to meet people than to get cut abs. The bandage on her arm caught her eye and reminded her why she was really there. She needed basic self-defense skills if she was going to walk the city alone.

She handed back her paperwork and made her way to the locker room. She had been smart that morning and worn her sports bra under her work clothes. With a quick glance around to make sure she was alone, she slipped her dress off and tossed on her tank top and shorts. It felt like high school gym class all over again. How old would she have to be before she finally felt comfortable in her skin?

She stuffed everything in the locker except the Tupperware container she had stashed in her bag, and then made her way to the classroom.

A stream of people filed out of the room. She stood back and waited for the rush to be over.

Mary came bouncing up and wrapped her arm around her shoulders. "I'm so glad you came!"

"I couldn't resist, you guys made it sound like fun." *And it was also a chance to see Mason again.*

"Let's get inside and get a good spot up front." Mary pulled her along.

Mason was facing the stereo, going through his phone. Mia set her stuff down and stood awkwardly for a minute. Her stomach dropped when Mason glanced up in the mirror and found her. He smiled broadly, set his phone down, and came right over to them. Mia was relieved he looked happy to see her. It meant he wasn't regretting the night before.

"Mary, Mia, how are you guys?" Mason glanced at Mia, then Mary, then back at Mia.

"We're pumped and ready for punishment." Mary laughed as she reached back and pulled her foot up towards her butt to stretch her leg.

Mia was suddenly regretting her decision. If she tried to grab her foot she would likely end up on the floor in a pile of twisted limbs. Coordination had never been her strong suit.

Remembering she had brought goodies, she leaned down and grabbed the Tupperware. "I made these for everyone. I know it goes against the point of working out in a gym, but it's what I'm good at." She shrugged and passed the box over to Mason.

She bounced on her toes nervously as he lifted the lid and revealed sugar cookies shaped like boxing gloves. She'd taken her time and iced each one individually, some had Raven's Haven on them, others had everyone's name.

"These are amazing." Mary gasped, "We left pretty late last night. How did you find the time to do this?" Mary grabbed the cookie with her name on it and bit off a piece.

"I had some pent-up energy I needed to get rid of." She shrugged and glanced at Mason.

The rest of the women came barging through the door, saving them from the awkwardness of the moment.

"Mia!" Multiple voices yelled out. She was quickly surrounded.

Mason and Mary took turns showing off the cookies. Mia blushed at the compliments being given to her. She wasn't used to so much attention.

"Let's save these for after class, though. I don't want anyone throwing up in the middle of our workout." Mason closed the lid and carried the box over to the stereo. "Line up ladies."

There were multiple groans and a few chuckles. Mia smiled. She knew every one of these women appreciated him and the class.

Mary pulled Mia up front and placed her dead center, in front of Mason. *It was probably best he saw how klutzy she was now, before she got too attached to him.*

The music kicked in and Mason transformed into a drill sergeant. Those demons they had battled last class were apparently not banished, because they worked their asses off. Grunts of determination and moans of exhaustion echoed around the room. But everyone, including her, gave everything they had.

At first, she looked pitiful compared to the rest of them, but Andy had come and helped her keep up. Mason had tried to help but every time he got close, she lost all sense of concentration and nearly took out everyone around her.

"Okay, ladies. It's that time." Mia glanced around as everyone walked to the mirror and stared themselves down. Mia's shoulders slumped. If this was going to be anything like the last time, it would be hard for her to listen to. But, she knew it was important for all of them. She walked to the end of the line so she could go last.

Maria was first. She balled her hands into fists and growled out her proclamation, "I will not let fear control me." Mia could feel the anger radiating off her.

Allison went next. "My wants matter."

Mia didn't think she sounded very convincing, but that was probably the point of the exercise. Say it until you believed it.

Tiny Tonya was next. She bit her lip as she stared herself up and down. Andy nodded at Tonya in the mirror. "You got this girl, go on."

The young girl smiled then forced herself to meet her own gaze in the mirror. "I am beautiful."

The entire line cheered their agreement. Mia teared up at seeing the girl's appreciation of her friend's support.

Jane's smile faded, she fiddled with the cuffs of her long sleeve shirt. After last night, Mia assumed that meant she was covering up something her husband had done to her. "I am worthy of love and admiration."

Lacey reached over and squeezed the other woman's hand, then turned to look at herself in the mirror. "I did nothing wrong." She let out a deep breath and smiled at the group.

Andy bent her neck side to side, amping herself up, "I am FREE!" Like before, Andy roared at herself in the mirror, then let out a huge laugh.

Next in line was Melissa, she was the only other girl in the class to wear long sleeves, and like Jane, she fiddled with them too. Mia wondered if they realized they did it. "I am more than my scars." A single tear slid down her cheek and she continued to stare at herself instead of glancing around.

Mason was next, Mia wondered what his would be. "I forgive myself."

Mia was surprised that his line was the same. Although this time he did sound a little more confident in his proclamation than he had the last time.

Kayla cleared her throat. "I can be free."

"Yeah, you can girl!" Andy pumped her fist in the air causing everyone to laugh.

Mary bit her lip nervously before looking at herself. "I am worthy of friends." She glanced shyly at the group.

Mia reached over and squeezed her new friends' hand. When she looked back at the mirror, she saw every pair of eyes focused on her. She stared at herself in the mirror. It was something she hadn't really done before. She could see every emotion she was feeling, it was a bit unnerving. She glanced over at Mason, who smiled encouragingly. With a deep breath, she turned back to her own demon and declared, "I am not what happened to me."

"Say it again." Mason nodded at Mia. "Mean it this time."

"I am *not* what happened to me!" Exhilaration coursed through her. It felt good to face herself for the first time since the attack.

The classroom erupted in cheers as Mia was engulfed in hugs from everyone except Mason, who high fived her. Mia didn't take offense. It was exactly how he responded to everyone in the class. She knew he was doing it out of respect, that's the kind of man he was.

# Fourteen

Mason ran the mop over the wood floor of the classroom, stalling while he waited for Mia to come out of the locker room. Each day he spent time with her was another day he felt more at peace than he had in a long time. Between her compassion for others, her humor, and intoxicating eyes, he was quickly finding he wanted to spend all his free time with her. Their kiss the other night sent his world spinning. He'd wanted to, but she got the nerve to do it first, which intrigued him even more. There was more depth to her than he first realized.

After the second pass of the room, she finally made her way toward the front. He tossed the mop in the closet and rushed out to meet her.

"Hey Mia, did you enjoy class? Is your arm doing okay?" His attention had been on her during the lesson and was relieved she was being careful with her injury and not pushing herself too quickly.

"I had a great time." She fiddled with the zipper of her gym bag. "I knew this place was special after I watched the first class, but after getting to know everyone a little more, I really get the importance of your work and the critical role you play in these women's lives." She blushed as she looked away.

"I get as much from this class as they do. I'm just glad you had fun." He grabbed his duffle bag from behind the check-in counter and walked with her towards the door. "I was thinking about ordering pizza and a movie. Interested in joining me?"

She walked through the door as he held it open for her. "As long as it's not a horror movie, I'm in."

"I'll do you one better, you can pick the movie and I promise I'll watch whatever you choose." He wasn't going to admit that he didn't watch horror movies either. Savannah was one of the most haunted cities in America. He had seen enough to know that shit is real, and he didn't want anything to do with any of it. "I'm guessing you walked from work?"

Mia nodded. "I'm parked around the corner, come on."

They spent the ride home in comfortable silence.

He pulled into the garage of the house and ran around the car to open her door. "Welcome to my humble abode."

He led her inside and waved towards the various rooms. His house was much smaller than hers, so there was no reason for a tour. He grabbed the T.V. remote off the coffee table and handed it to her. "I think it's only fair that I should get to shower since you did at the gym. You can scroll through and get the movie queued up while I'm in there. Also, I'll order the pizza before I get in, any special requests?"

Mia plopped down on the couch. "I'm not a veggie girl. I usually eat cheese, but I'm good with any of the meats too."

"Cheese is good for me. I'll pay online, it shouldn't get here before I'm out, but if it does feel free to get the door." Mason chuckled as Mia gave him a mock salute.

He stopped at the door to his bedroom and glanced back. Seeing her cuddled up watching T.V. felt right to him. He shook his head and turned away. How did this small girl slip past all his defenses and plant herself so firmly in his heart?

# Fifteen

Mia looked calm on the outside but inside she was doing a jig. She was in Mason's house and he was naked in the other room right now. Soon he would be cuddled up on the couch next to her. Life had never been so perfect.

The doorbell pulled her out of her musings. She glanced at the clock. *That was the fastest pizza delivery ever.* She jumped up and swung the door open with a smile, which quickly turned to confusion.

An older couple stared at her in surprise. "Um, hello?" Mia wasn't sure what to say.

"Is Mason home?" The woman's brittle smile made Mia uneasy. The man was studying Mia intensely.

"Mother, Father? What are you doing here?" Mason asked from behind her.

Mia spun around.

"May we come in?" His father's icy question made goosebumps rise on Mia's arms.

Mason turned and walked back to the living room. "Give me a minute." Mia's face flushed as she finally noticed he only had a towel wrapped around his waist. *Damn his parents for being there.*

Mia shuffled behind them to the kitchen table. "Hi, I'm Mia. Sorry for the awkward greeting before. I was expecting the pizza we ordered."

The couple didn't respond.

Mason joined them, he stood directly behind Mia. "Why are you here?"

Mia's heart broke as the older woman's eyes filled with tears. "You haven't returned our calls, you know what tomorrow is. I want us all together."

Mason's hands were gripped into tight fists, "And what if I don't want to be with you on the anniversary of my sister's death?" Mason said sarcastically. She reached back and grabbed his hand. He hadn't told her about the anniversary, maybe because he didn't want to be comforted. But right now, she could hear the pain in his voice and desperately wanted to console him.

"I'm sorry you wasted your time coming over here. Mia and I have plans tonight and tomorrow."

The news surprised Mia, but she was happy to play along. The doorbell rang, cutting through the tense silence. "I'll get it." She all but ran for the door.

Mia was overly thrilled to see the teenager holding the pizza box. "Good evening, Ma'am. I have a large cheese pizza and a two liter of coke?" Mia hadn't bothered to find out exactly what he ordered, so she went with it.

"Sounds right. And how are you tonight?" She stepped out onto the porch and closed the door. The sound of angry voices echoed around the house.

"Um, good I guess?" Mia realized she was making the poor kid uncomfortable in her attempt to avoid the confrontation happening inside.

"Well, I'll take that from you and let you go." She grabbed the box and soda and went back inside. Not wanting to interrupt the intense family conversation in the other room, she went to the living room and sat on the couch.

Her mouth watered as the smell of the pizza reached her nose.

Mason's mother walked in the room, she didn't even glance toward Mia as she continued walking to the door. Between clenched teeth she said, "Mia, it was nice meeting you."

Mia didn't even see his father leave.

Mason collapsed next to her on the couch, the palms of his hands pressed into his eyes. "I am so sorry about that. I had no idea they were going to show up. They weren't trying to be rude to you, it's a rough time right now and I think it took them by surprise that I had someone here."

"How are you doing considering what tomorrow is?" Mia knew she was taking a risk by making him talk about it.

"I've been avoiding thinking about it. I was hoping not to face it until tomorrow, but they had to come and ruin that too." Mason's voiced cracked from the grief threatening to choke him.

"I'm not sure what you had planned, but I can call in tomorrow if you want company?" Mia knew she would hate to be alone if she were in his place, but being a guy, maybe he preferred it.

Mason's hands dropped onto his lap. He turned and looked at her. The pain in his eyes crushed her. "Normally I go sit at her grave and read to her. I don't stop until my throat is raw." Tears welled in Mia's eyes at the image of Mason sitting at his sister's gravestone. "It doesn't matter how many years go by, it always hurts as much as it did when it first happened." His hands fisted, "I wish I knew if it was ever going to get easier."

Mia grabbed his hand and uncurled his fingers from digging into his palm. "It won't get easier until you are ready to stop torturing yourself. I'm sorry if that sounds mean, but I haven't known you long and even I can see what you put yourself through. Your sister would never want this life for you." She reached up and rested her hand against his face, her thumb lightly brushed away the tear that had escaped. "Maybe tomorrow we should treat it as a celebration of the life she had and go to her favorite places?"

Mia held her breath. She had no idea how he would respond to her bluntness.

He stared into her eyes. She could see the wheels turning in his head. "This may sound crazy, but I think she brought you to me, you are exactly what I need."

Mia's heart swelled. Forgetting her shyness, she leaned up on her knees and straddled his lap. "Let me make you feel better." She pulled her shirt off and tossed it aside. She heard his intake of breath right before she leaned down and kissed him.

# *Sixteen*

Mason's eyes fluttered open. His mind knew immediately what day it was but for the first time in years, his heart was happy. He glanced down. Mia was wrapped in his arms, her breathing slow and steady.

The night before had gone from good to really bad to amazing. He had hoped for a relaxing night getting closer with Mia. But that was derailed when he stepped out of the shower and heard his mother's voice.

They'd been leaving him messages for the last week, asking if he was coming home for Raven's Anniversary. He had ignored every one of them. He understood they lost their child and needed to grieve, but he also understood that they took money in exchange for their silence. He wasn't ready to forgive them for that betrayal.

Mia yawned then smiled up at Mason. "Morning." Her hair was covering half her face and her eyes still had the soft look of sleep in them. He thought it was adorable.

"How long have you been awake? You look bright eyed and bushy tailed."

Mason laughed, "Do people actually say that? And for the record, I woke up about a minute before you did."

"So, you look this good all the time?" Mia asked in mock exasperation.

"You think I look good?" He gave her a cheesy smile.

Mia rolled her eyes. "Now you're just fishing for compliments."

"It never hurts to get a compliment." Mason shrugged.

Mia leaned up on one arm so she was face to face with him. "Then please allow me to say you look good enough to eat."

Mason opened his mouth to reply when Mia's stomach growled. "Apparently, you aren't kidding. I better get you breakfast before you turn cannibalistic on me."

"Can we stop at my house before we go out so I can get clean clothes?"

"Sure, let me rinse off in the shower and we'll head out." Mia laid back and relaxed as Mason hopped out of bed and walked to the bathroom. He could feel her eyes on him and hoped she was enjoying the show.

As the water ran down his back it dawned on him just how happy he was. This was normally such a dark day, but thanks to Mia he was eager to share his sister's memory. Maybe it wasn't time that healed wounds but people.

He dried off quickly and was slightly disappointed to see Mia was no longer in the bedroom. He was hoping to give her another show.

"Yes sir, I'll see you tomorrow." Mason walked out dressed and ready to go as Mia was hanging up her cell phone.

"I called work and let them know I wasn't coming in, so you have me as long as you want me around." Mia walked up and wrapped her arms around his waist. "If at any time you want to be alone, let me know. You won't hurt my feelings."

"I appreciate the offer but I'm actually feeling pretty good." He leaned down and kissed her softly. "Let's get you home and changed so we can get breakfast." Mason stopped dead in his tracks as he was about to step out the door.

Mia had to stop hard to avoid slamming into his back. "What's wrong?"

He spun around. "We said we were going to go to Raven's favorite places today. It dawned on me that the cafe where I met you is where we were going to go for breakfast. I realize now it was stupid of me to take you there." Mason rubbed his forehead, he felt like an idiot. He was glad that he realized it *now,* and not as they were pulling up to the restaurant.

Mia grabbed his hand and squeezed. "It's okay, I don't associate the cafe with what happened to me. If anything, I should be happy to go back there since it's where I met you." She pulled him towards his car. "Besides, today is about Raven, so show me what she was like."

Mason still wasn't convinced they should go to the restaurant, but he appreciated Mia going along anyway. Maybe today would be a good day.

# Seventeen

Mia showered and dressed quickly, leaving Mason in front of the T.V.

When she came back into the living room, she found him on a step stool fixing one of the shelves in the pantry. She stood silently for a minute, enjoying the view, before clearing her throat. "I guess you didn't find anything good to watch?"

Mason smacked his elbow against the wall as he spun around with a guilty expression. "Ow...it started out innocent enough. I noticed you had a lightbulb out in the hallway, which led me to find the lightbulbs, and that's when I found the broken shelf. I may have also tightened a few loose screws on the cabinet handles in the kitchen." He stepped down and handed her the screwdriver. "That was intrusive, wasn't it? I'm sorry."

She laughed at the guilty expression on his face. "Don't be sorry. I've been glaring at that shelf for two months now, pissed it wouldn't magically fix itself. I admit I didn't learn any of this stuff before moving out. I realize now I took advantage of how easily my parents took care of these things." Mia put the screwdriver in the drawer and grabbed her purse. "Don't tell my dad, but I actually had to Google how to shut off the water when the toilet overflowed. I'm quite proud of how much I have learned since being on my own. But as you can see, there is still a lot more for me to master."

"While I one hundred percent believe women can do anything men can do, I also believe you shouldn't have to. Especially not while you are down one arm." Mason held the front door open for her. "Maybe this weekend you can give me a list of things that need fixing and I'll see what I can do?' He leaned down and whispered in her ear. "And between you and me, I've had to Google tons of stuff, fixing things doesn't come naturally just because I was born a male."

"Valid point, how very sexist of me to assume otherwise." She kissed his cheek as he held the car door open for her. "The least I can do is feed you while you work."

"It's a date." He winked before shutting the door.

Mia's gaze followed him as he walked around the car, still struggling to believe she was out with him. She had tried describing him to her mom and friends back home, but she knew she hadn't done him justice. Hopefully, there would be an opportunity to get a picture of him while they were out today. Her friends were going to freak when they saw how hot he was.

"What's so funny?" Mason asked as he slid in the car and caught her giggling to herself.

"Don't mind me, I entertain myself quite easily." Mia grinned. "We need to eat soon or you are going to see my hangry side, and I can't be held responsible for what happens after that."

He put the car in reverse and looked over his shoulder as he backed out. "Yes ma'am, let's go."

They drove in peaceful silence. Mia thought it was nice that neither felt the need to fill the silence with meaningless conversation.

As they made their way up the sidewalk it dawned on her that she had been avoiding the area since the attack. Luckily, Mason was the perfect person to help her face any demons that might pop up.

She kept her head down and walked quickly, sliding into the first open booth. As she reached for the menu, her fingers cramped. Her hands had been balled into fists, and her shoulders were tense. She shook them to release the tension.

"Are you okay? We can leave if you want. Trust me, my sister had lots of places she loved to eat."

Mia felt guilty that he was focusing on her. "I'm good. Now, what would Raven have told me to eat?" She set the menu down, determined to order whatever it was.

"I'm not sure you want it, it's sickeningly sweet." She cocked her eyebrow at him and waited. "I warned you...she always got the cinnamon roll pancakes and a side of bacon."

"Is it more like a cinnamon roll or a pancake?" She thought it sounded awesome either way.

He sat forward, his eyes bright and sparkling. "It's pancakes with cinnamon chips baked in them and icing slathered on top. It's no joke, I can eat one if I'm lucky, but she could take down a stack with no problem."

She tapped her fingers on the table top, deciding whether she could eat something so sickeningly sweet. "Challenge accepted." Mia smiled as the waitress walked up. "I'll have the cinnamon roll pancakes, a side of bacon, and a hot tea."

Mason handed the menus over to the waitress. "I'll have the same thing, but with coffee."

"I thought you weren't a fan?"

He shrugged. "I'm not, but it's not about me today."

"Do you have a picture of her?" Mia had looked around his house but hadn't seen any family pictures anywhere.

Mason reached into his back pocket and pulled out his wallet. He pulled a folded photo out of the billfold and passed it over. "It's the last picture I have of us together."

Mia opened the paper; her fingers traced the worn creases. It was obvious he looked at it often.

"The last football game of the season was always senior night; our families escorted us across the field."

Mia wanted to study the slightly younger looking Mason in his uniform, but her attention was drawn to the young girl he had his arm around.

Raven looked almost identical to him except she barely reached his shoulders, and was as pale as he was tan. She was beautiful. Tears welled in her eyes seeing Raven smiling up at her big brother in the picture. Mia tried to see if she could see the girl's pain or secret, but there wasn't anything obvious. She imagined Mason likely studied this picture looking for the same thing, wondering how he had missed the signs.

Mia gently folded the photo and handed it back. "She was beautiful, it's a great picture."

Mason nodded but didn't say a word. Mia could tell he was trying to control his emotions.

They were saved from the awkward silence by the food arriving. Mia's eyes bulged at the plate in front of her. "Oh my god, you said the icing was slathered on and you weren't kidding. It's more like can I get some pancakes to go along with my icing."

Mason laughed at her joke as he quickly wiped a single tear from the corner of his eye. "Dig in, you are about to go into a sugar coma.

Maybe instead of walking around after this, we should drive, you have no idea how heavy those things sit in your stomach."

Mia picked up her silverware and nodded down at the plate. "If Raven could do it, then so can we." She put the first decadent bite in her mouth and moaned. It was not going to be a hardship to eat every bite. It was incredible. Raven had great taste in breakfast food. Mia couldn't wait to experience more of Raven's favorite things.

# *Eighteen*

After breakfast, Mason drove Mia around town. She hadn't lived in the area long, so she only knew her immediate neighborhood and the tourist areas. He surprised himself when he found himself driving by his parent's house. He wanted her to see the house he and Raven grew up in.

Mia rolled down the window so she could stick her head out and see all of it. "Wow, and you said my house was big, this place is a mansion."

Mason's eyes unfocused as he looked straight ahead at the road. "It was a fun house to grow up in. I don't miss it though." He rested his head back against the headrest and stared straight ahead. "I haven't stepped back inside since I moved out. I can't, every room of that house has a memory with Raven in it, and my brain betrays me every time by replaying them over and over again."

Mia laid her hand on top of his. "Thank you for showing me this. I love getting to see where you grew up."

Mason wanted the suffocating feelings to go away. He took a deep breath, then cleared his throat. "Up next, we go to the *Book Lady Bookstore*."

Mia squirmed in excitement, "You don't have to drag me there. I am happy to go to a bookstore anytime."

On the drive back to the historic area of the city, Mason pointed out facts and stories about places they drove by. He wasn't a great tour guide, but he knew enough to be slightly entertaining.

They lucked out with a close parking spot. Mason led Mia inside the store. The smell of old books invaded their senses. He didn't have a respect for it until he started trying to get closer to Raven. "Have a look around, I'm going to grab a few things and I'll meet you up front in a bit."

Mia barely nodded as she immediately turned and wandered off. He recognized the signs. She'd forgotten all about him and zeroed in on the books...There could be worse things to come in second too.

## Nineteen

Mia had never been in the presence of so many out of print books. She loved that the store had more than just new authors.

She grabbed a few books and found her way to the checkout counter. Mason was grabbing bags from the clerk. "I didn't realize you were such an avid reader." Her eyes widened to see how many books were in the two large bags.

"I'm not, these are all children's books. Tomorrow I'll drop them off at the elementary school Raven and I went to."

Mia didn't say a word. Her book lust quickly switched to sexual lust. She was falling for him fast, and the idea scared her. She'd never really had a serious relationship before and suddenly she was wishing she could be in his bed every night. She needed to clear her head before she jumped him right where he stood. "You're a modern-day saint." He shook his head to disagree. "So, what's next?"

He stood back and let her checkout. "Let's head over to Tybee Island for lunch."

Mia paid for her books. Mason grabbed her bag and carried it for her.

She could get used to having him around.

On the car ride to the restaurant Mason hummed quietly along to the radio. Mia was lost in thought as she flipped through one of her new books.

"Okay, we're here."

Mia glanced up to see the largest plaster made crab she had ever seen hanging over the entrance. She suddenly regretted agreeing to eat whatever Raven did, Mia did not like seafood.

"This place was on that show *Deadliest Catch* a few years ago. They are known for their Alaskan King Crab."

Mia's stomach rolled. She wasn't sure she could go through with it.

She followed him inside, pleasantly surprised by how cute it was. They were led to a large outdoor patio right on the water. "After we eat, we can check out the lagoon, they have something crazy like seventy alligators you can feed."

"Hi, welcome to *The Crab Shack*, what can I get you to drink?" The waiter smiled at them both, then waited for Mia to order first.

"I'll have a sweet tea."

"Same for me." Mason nodded at the waiter before turning back to the menu. "What looks good?"

Mia studied the pages in front of her. It was ninety percent seafood. "I was thinking the roast chicken."

"No crab or lobster?" Mia peaked up to see him studying her.

She crunched her face. "I don't actually eat seafood."

Mason's head fell back as he groaned. "I should have thought of that, I'm sorry I didn't ask."

Mia reached forward and squeezed his hand. "Don't be, all seafood restaurants have food for us weirdos."

"What don't you like about it? Is it the taste?" Mason looked genuinely curious.

"Well, I haven't actually tried it before. It's more the idea of it that grosses me out."

Mason's jaw dropped. "Seriously, well that's crazy to not like something you haven't tried." He scanned the menu for a second before glancing back up. "Okay, you order the chicken. I'm going to get the sampler platter and if you are feeling adventurous, you can try some of my food, no pressure though!"

Mia bit her lip as she considered his offer. "No promises, but I'll consider it."

The waiter returned and took their orders.

Mia finally got up the nerve to ask for the picture she desperately wanted. "The water is really beautiful. Do you mind taking a selfie with me so I can send it to my parents? It's okay if you don't want to, but they are still so afraid for me and I want to show them I'm fine."

He smiled wide, "Sure, we can do a few by the water, then later I think we can hold the gators and take pictures too, come on." Mason hopped up from his chair and waited for Mia to do the same.

She grabbed her phone and walked the short distance to the edge of the patio so they'd only have water behind them.

Mason leaned against the railing waiting for her to stand next to him. "Do your parents know about us? I mean will they freak if I have my arms around you?"

Mia's stomach did a little flip when he said 'us', she hadn't wanted to assume too much, but his words made it sound like he thought they were together. "They know we've been hanging out and wouldn't read too much into you having your arm around me."

"So, they don't know I'm your boyfriend?" He stood there giving her a hopeful look.

*Shut the front door*, he said boyfriend. "I wasn't sure what we were, they know we've gone out a few times."

"Well, okay then." Mason pulled her against his chest, wrapped his arm around her, and held his phone out. She wrapped her arms around his waist and smiled. It was probably the largest smile she'd ever had and would look ridiculous in the picture, but she couldn't tone it down if she tried.

He snapped multiple pics before shifting so he was standing behind her with one arm hooked around her stomach. On impulse, she turned and kissed his cheek as he pushed the button.

"Excuse me, your food is here." The waiter waved towards their table to show the plates ready to go.

"Thank you." Mason grabbed her hand and walked with her back to the table.

"Wow, that is a huge platter!" Mia had never seen so many types of seafood on one plate before.

"Let me know if any of it looks good to try." She watched as he fiddled with his phone for a few minutes.

"There, it's official." He turned his phone around to show her his Instagram account. He had posted the photos with the comment: *Every day is a good day when your girlfriend is in your arms.* "Hopefully it's okay, it automatically shares to Facebook too."

She flipped through the album. She almost didn't recognize the girl looking back at her. "These came out great, I'll share them and it will be official on my side, too."

She handed the phone back and grabbed hers. With a few taps on the screen she had shared both posts. Her friends were going to blow up her phone. She tossed it in her purse so it wouldn't distract them, then grabbed her silverware.

"So..." Mason waved towards his platter.

"Did Raven eat all of those?" She held back a shiver of disgust as she stared down at the creatures, some still had legs attached.

Mason barked out a giant laugh, "You look completely horrified." He held his side as he tried to stop laughing. "Yes, she did but you don't have to try any of it."

Mia blew out a loud sigh. "I'll try a small piece of the crab, but I'm not breaking a leg to get to it. I am not touching the mussels or the crawfish."

Mason set his napkin on his laugh. "You look like you are about to be tortured. Raven would probably have loved to see you squirm. But honestly, don't put yourself through it if it's that gross to think about."

She shook her head and waved at him to get her a piece. "No, it's okay. I'm doing this, now bust a kneecap on that thing and let me get this over with."

"Technically they don't have kneecaps, but I got you." He winked before going to work.

A minute later he passed his fork over with a tiny piece of meat on it. "Dunk it in the butter, trust me, it's all about the butter."

Mia stared at the chunk, trying hard not to gag. With a heavy sigh, she swirled it in the butter, dunked it in and out a couple of times, then closed her eyes and popped it in her mouth.

She chewed a couple of time before swallowing and opened her eyes to find Mason staring at her. "It's sweeter than I expected, it's a little soft for meat, but it's not bad."

"Want another piece?" He held his hand out to get his fork back.

She held her hands up. "I'll stick with my chicken. It's not just seafood that grosses me out. Honestly, if I gave chicken and red meat enough thought, I wouldn't be able to eat them, but I'm choosing ignorance for the sake of my appetite."

"No judgement here, I get it." He cracked another crab leg and focused on his food.

Mia grabbed her phone and took a picture in snapchat of him with the giant leg in his hand with the caption: *It takes a gorgeous guy to get me to try crab.*

She posted the pic, ignored the texts from her friends, and put her phone back in her purse. Today was about Mason.

# Twenty

After lunch, Mason drove to the beach. Raven had loved to watch the sunset, unfortunately, they couldn't stay that long.

He laid a blanket on the sand and sat. Mia gracefully curled up beside him and leaned into his side. He should have been feeling melancholy and contemplating what Raven would be like if she were still alive which is what he would normally have done on her anniversary. Instead, he was feeling content and excited for the future, all because of the tiny woman in his arms. He had no idea how much easier this day would have been if he shared it with someone else. An image of his parents briefly flashed in his mind. His anger quickly pushed them back out. He wasn't ready for that yet.

Mia glanced up at him. "Do you ever see any of Raven's friends?"

He shrugged, "Yeah, I run into them sometimes. They're always sweet and ask me how I'm doing." He absentmindedly leaned down and kissed the top of her head. "Her best friend had a really rough time after it happened. She blamed herself almost as much as I did. She was in therapy for a while, I heard she's doing better."

Mia nuzzled her face into the side of his neck. "It's sad to think how many people are affected by suicide."

He nodded and fell silent as they listened to the waves.

After a while he sighed heavily and broke the spell they were in. "I've got to get to the gym, we've got class this evening. Are you up for going or do you want me to take you home?"

Mia groaned at Mason's question. She was still full from lunch and couldn't imagine doing any physical activity but she couldn't skip on Raven's day.

"If we swing by my house, I'll change into gym clothes and ride in with you. If you have things to do before class I can work out on the machines."

"Sounds like a plan." He hopped up from the sand and held his hands out to help her up.

Once she had cleaned herself off and helped him fold the blanket, he laced his fingers with hers.

He hadn't meant to say the *B* word at lunch, and had been torturing himself all day with how to broach the relationship subject with her. The photo gave him the perfect excuse, but instead of asking her what she thought they were outright he declared it then hoped she didn't protest.

"I had a great day today, thank you for letting me tag along." Mia smiled up at him.

He stopped and turned her to face him. "You have no idea how much you helped me today. I should be thanking you." He leaned down and kissed her softly on the lips. "You made a bad day good again."

## Twenty-One

Mason held the door of the gym open for Mia. "Do you want to sit in my office while I get some paperwork done before class?"

Mia glanced around and saw the Hispanic girl, Maria, from class working on a machine in the back corner. "I'm good, I'm going to go hang with Maria."

Mason kissed her on the cheek and made his way to the office. Maria glanced up and found Mia in the mirror. She smiled and waved.

Like the other times, Mia had seen her, she was wearing a shirt and shorts three sizes too big for her. It was obviously some kind of cover or shield, and made Mia sad to see her hiding.

Mia sat at the machine next to her and adjusted the weights. "Hey Maria, how are you?"

"I'm good, I got off work early so thought I would get some extra work in." She did a few reps on the leg press before turning back to Mia. "Was it a trick of the mirror or did I see Mason kissing you?"

Mia knew her face had to be glowing red. She wasn't sure how this group of women was going to take it with her swooping in and taking the guy. "Yeah, we've been seeing a lot of each other the last few days."

"That's good, I'm glad he's found someone." Maria focused ahead again and did ten more reps.

"What about you, do you have someone?" Mia instantly regretted her question. The anger that overtook Maria was shocking and scary.

She bit her lip and waited while Maria muttered a few sentences in Spanish, none of which Mia understood.

"I'm sorry, I didn't mean anything by my question." Mia was suddenly wishing Mason would come and interrupt them.

Maria closed her eyes and sighed heavily. "It's not you, I'm still dealing with my issues and the strangest things will set me off." She pushed through another ten reps before turning back to Mia. "After I dropped out of school and moved back home, I did get better. As soon as I think I'm in a good place I have one of these episodes as I call them and it takes me right back to the night of my attack."

Mia wasn't sure what to say. She didn't want to apologize again but she felt terrible for setting her off. "I didn't know, I shouldn't have pried. I am so sorry."

Mia could see the stress lines were starting to smooth out on the other girl's face and her shoulders relaxed a little. "It's not your fault. You aren't psychic, so how would you know an innocent question like that could be a problem?" She stood up and started wiping down the machine. "Besides, it's time for class so I can get out all this aggression."

Mia wiped down her machine and followed Maria toward the classroom. A screech behind her had her ducking as arms wrapped around her neck.

"Oh my God. I saw your snapchat. You and Mason?" Mary was beaming as she squeezed the air from Mia's lungs.

"I'm as surprised as you are. I figured he would want to keep it casual, but he called himself my boyfriend. I almost passed out." All three girls laughed. Mia forgot how good it felt to relax with friends and talk about silly things like if a boy likes you.

"What's so funny?" Mason walked up to the group, causing all three of them to laugh even harder.

"Nothing at all, Romeo." Mary winked and pushed by him to set her stuff down.

As the rest of the class filed in there were a few wolf whistles and high fives, apparently, news traveled fast.

"Okay ladies, the fun is over. Get up here and let's get moving." Mason pushed a button on his phone and music blared through the speakers.

Mia loved that he was all business when it came to this class and the women he was helping empower.

## Twenty-Two

After the group lined up and said their truths the class should have been over, but Mason felt the day needed to be recognized.

"Ladies, thank you for everything you have given to this class. You are the hardest working, most badass women I know. Today is the anniversary of Raven's death." He paused to let the ripple of surprise from around the room quiet down. "Seeing how much you gave tonight reminds me why I do this. You honor Raven's memory by being here and supporting this gym."

He hadn't meant to get emotional, but he felt the lump in his throat threatening to strangle him. He stood frozen as the group surrounded him into a big group hug. For the most part, these women didn't like to be touched so he normally stuck to high fives. To have them embrace him and each other was a huge sign that all of them were starting to heal, even if only a little bit.

Andy stepped back first. "I'm sure the rest of the group would agree with me when I say we should be thanking you. I was a weak, broken woman when I found this place. You literally saved my life and gave me hope again."

The rest of the group started talking at once. Mason was overwhelmed at their words.

"Ladies, you are amazing and always an inspiration to me. I'd love to stay and chat but I have a lesson starting in a few minutes." He thanked each of them individually as he held the door open for them. The last in line was Mia.

She fiddled with the strings of her gym bag. "I know it's been a long day for you. I understand if you want to crash tonight, but I was thinking I could wait around for you, then we can get dinner and hang at my place?"

Mason was relieved she asked him first. He really didn't want to be alone tonight, but was afraid he was overwhelming her. "Honestly, if you can put up with me for a bit longer, I would love the distraction from my own thoughts."

She held her bag up towards him. "I always have a book with me. I'll go sit at the coffee shop around the corner and you text me when you're done, then we can go have dinner?"

"It's a date. Do you want me to have someone walk with you?" He knew she hadn't walked alone at night since the attack and didn't want to put her in an uncomfortable situation because of him.

"Are you kidding me, look at these muscles. I can defend myself now." She flexed an arm, that had no definition in it, but he still loved that she had the confidence to take care of herself.

"How could I have ever doubted you, be careful and I'll text when I'm done." He kissed her and watched her leave.

## Twenty-Three

Mia tried to read while she sat waiting for Mason, but all she could think about was how he had lost his sister and his parents in a very short time. He had built a wall of guilt around himself and hadn't let anyone inside in years.

It was obvious when his parents had shown up that they were hoping to make amends. If he looked at it from their perspective, they lost both their children. Mia saw the hope that was in his mom's eyes when she first got there.

After torturing herself for a few seconds, she finally gave in to her thoughts and decided she was going to push her luck again and try to get Mason to see his parents.

She went up to the counter and ordered a mix of pastries, then sat and pulled her book out. Now that she had a plan she could relax and wait for his text.

***

Mia had heard the phone vibrating next to her but she was in the middle of a particularly riveting scene in her book and couldn't stop herself from finishing the chapter.

Out of the corner of her eye Mia saw someone running by the window and into the café.

"Oh my god, there you are." An out of breath Mason was standing above her looking pale.

"What's wrong? Why do you look panicked?" Mia's mind was still partially in the book and she was not quite making sense of his concern.

"I texted, then waited, and texted a few more times." He plopped into the seat across from her. "My mind went to the worst place. I thought maybe something had happened."

Mia frowned. "I am so sorry. I did warn you I get sucked into books for hours. My bad." She gave her most angelic smile and hoped he wasn't really that mad. How would she talk him into seeing his parents if he was in a bad mood?

"It's fine, I shouldn't have jumped to conclusions." He lifted the lid of the pastry box and peeked inside. "Is this dinner?"

"Actually-" Under the table, she was wringing her hands, "I thought we could take this over to your parents and spend the last couple of hours of Raven's anniversary with them?" She paled at the emotions crossing his face. "I don't think Raven would want this. She wouldn't want you isolated and she wouldn't want her parents having lost both their children. Maybe it's time for you to help each other heal. You don't have to fix everything tonight, but maybe take the first step?" She held her breath until she thought she might pass out.

He stared at her for a full minute, she felt a bead of sweat roll down her back. Finally, he broke the silence. "You have turned everything upside down in the last twenty-four hours, everything I normally do, you challenged and changed."

Mia's stomach dropped, she had pushed her luck a step too far. "I'm sorry, I should've minded my own business."

He held his hand up to stop her. "But you've been right about everything so far. I know I'm not ready to forgive them, but if you are going to be with me, I promise I'll give it a try. Let's grab some tacos down the street, then go over okay?"

Mia slumped against her chair. She thought she had screwed up the first real relationship she'd ever had. She stood and held her hand out to him, "I'm with you, every step of the way."

## Twenty-Four

Mason's hand shook as he reached up to knock on his parent's front door.

The door opened and his mother looked shocked to see them standing there. "Mason?"

Mason stood frozen, the two sides of his brain warring with each other. One part of him was screaming to run away and protect Mia from them. The other side was forcing him to remember that this was his mother. She was the woman who cuddled with him when he cried, cheered for him at every game he played in, and helped him when he struggled in school. She was always patient and loving but still...

Mia cleared her throat and smiled at the older woman. "Hi again, I hope we're not disturbing you. We thought we would take you up on the offer to spend some time together tonight."

"We brought dessert." Mason mindlessly held the box up. It had been so long since they had spoken, he was struggling to function. Thank God for Mia running interference.

He could see the hope light up in his mom's eyes. Maybe Mia was right. It was time to make amends.

His mother stood back to let them in. "Yes, of course, come in. Show yourselves to the family room, I'll get your father."

Mia pulled him along. She was his strength, his light, trying to bring him out of the darkness. His mother closed the door and all but ran upstairs.

Mia smiled up at him. "Show me around."

As he showed her around she pointed at family photos and asked when they were taken.

At first, his responses were robotic, but once the memories started flooding in, he became more animated as he described the events taking place in each picture.

They made their way to the family room and sat on the couch. He wrapped his arms around her shoulders and pulled her close.

It didn't take long for his parents to join them. His father walked over and sat on the chair across from them. "Mason, Mia." He nodded and didn't say another word.

"I'm so happy you both came over, how was your day?" Mason's mother tried her best to make the intensity of the situation lessen.

Mia turned and looked to him. Apparently, she was done coddling him.

He cleared his throat, hoping his voice would come out strong. "We had a great day. Mia had the idea to celebrate Raven by visiting her favorite places. Then we went to the gym for class, had a quick bite, and now we're here."

Mia quirked an eyebrow at him, obviously, she didn't like his underwhelming description.

His mother smiled, "That sounds wonderful. I wish we had thought of that. I guess we know why we didn't see you at the cemetery today."

Mason cocked his head sideways, his eyebrows scrunched in confusion. "You went there today? Why now?"

"We go every year but we didn't want to bother you, so we always stayed back and left you to grieve in peace. Once you left we'd go over and say our own words to her." His mother's eyes glistened with unshed tears.

"I never saw you there before." He wasn't sure if he should believe her.

She wiped a single tear from her cheek. "You don't know how beautiful and painful it was to sit there, watching you read to her."

Mason struggled to comprehend what he was hearing. He glanced at his father who stared at the coffee table with a stony look on his face. He was not the same man from his childhood. This was a much harder, angrier man.

"It sounds like you have been very good for our son, where did you meet?" Mia perked up at his mother's question.

"Actually, your son saved me from being attacked, then I started going to his self-defense classes." She rubbed the bandage on her arm.

His mother clapped her hands together. "I've read a lot about your gym, it sounds like you've been doing a lot of good things there."

He gave her credit; his mother was trying.

Mia squeezed his hand and smiled at him. "You should come see it, he has thank you cards from all kinds of people and there is this group of women in the self-defense class that are amazing, and that is mostly because of him. He gives every piece of himself in those classes, trying to help as many people as possible." Mason's face heated at her praise.

"I've been there a few times." Everyone turned stunned faces towards his father, who continued staring at the table. "I've taken the tour and once you were there teaching a class. Raven would be so proud to see what you've done."

Mason's mind reeled. He had no idea his dad had ever been there, let alone watched him teach. He thought he'd be angry, knowing his father stepped foot into his gym. But, oddly enough, it made him feel better.

He had no idea how to respond, so he took the easy way out and grabbed the tray of food. "Pastry?" Mason could see his father was equally relieved that the emotional discussion was being avoided.

The stubborn older man grabbed a scone from the box and sat back.

Out of the corner of his eye, he saw Mia and his mom shake their heads at each other. He imagined they were silently saying, *boys*.

## Twenty-Five

"Well that wasn't so bad was it?" Mia glanced over at Mason as they drove away from his parent's house.

He reached over and grabbed her hand. "Thank you for making me do this. It's not perfect, but it's a step in the right direction.

"What did you think when your dad said he'd been to the gym?" Mia had been dying to ask him that question since his dad made the revelation.

"Honestly, I was shocked, I had no idea. It made me feel a little better knowing that they had been going to the cemetery and following what I'm doing with the gym." He chuckled quietly, "I didn't realize how much I'd missed them until now, and I have you to thank for that. All these years I've been trying to make amends for what I did, but today is the first time I've felt like maybe I've done enough, and Raven is looking down on me, proud of what I have done in her name." Mason reached up and wiped a tear from his cheek.

Mia's heart swelled. It felt good knowing she had a small part in helping him heal. "You've done enough. You can stop blaming yourself and continue doing what you do best, championing for those who need someone to believe in them and show them how to be brave."

Mason cupped her cheek. "I think Raven did send you to me. I think she wants me to know I can stop fighting for forgiveness."

✳✳✳

Mason and the rest of the gang from Raven's Haven will be back soon. Sign up for my newsletter to get updates on new releases:

http://eepurl.com/bwq4MX

# ~Other Books by the Author~

Loving the Monster Within

Reviving Love

Sassy Mates: In My Mate's Sight

Sassy Mates: In My Mate's Defense

Paranormal Dating Agency: My Oath To You

Broken Dreams

Forever Yours, Casey

The Laird's Promise

To Steal a Prince's Heart

The Love's Protector Series

Awakening Her Desires

The Evolution of Sam

Finding His Swing

Wicked Wonderland Retreat Box Set

Sexy In White (An O My! Novel)

# The Black Hollow Series

The town of Black Hollow has many stories to tell. Please visit the website and join the Facebook group to know when the next story is releasing.

https://www.blackhollowtown.com/
https://www.facebook.com/blackhollowtown/

Books in the Black Hollow Series
(In order by Publication Date)

Loving the Monster Within (Prequel)
*by Cassidy K. O'Connor*

Reviving Love *by Cassidy K. O'Connor*

*Silver Linings by Sheri Lyn*

*Finding Her Fire by Gracen Miller*

*One Man's Curse by Jennifer Wedmore*

# ABOUT THE AUTHOR

Cassidy lives in the Tampa, Florida area with her high school sweetheart, their three children, two crazy dogs, a guinea pig and a skinny pig. She loves reading and going to the movies but not nearly as much as she enjoys watching her kids either playing ball or performing with one of their instruments. She also loves to travel and hopes to one day watch a baseball game in every MLB stadium in the country.

To learn more about Cassidy please visit her online at www.cassidykoconnor.com.

You can also find her on Facebook at www.facebook.com/cassidykoconnorauthor

She always welcomes new friends and encourages readers to reach out to her.

# Excerpt from
# Forever Yours, Casey

## Chapter One

## Brittany

I can taste the bile rising in my throat as soon as I hear the knock on my door. I've been expecting them but I'm still shaking as I reach for the doorknob. Standing in the doorway are two police officers. I recognize them from the diner and I can tell they aren't happy about doing this either.

"Morning, ma'am. We have a warrant for your arrest."

My shoulders sag in resignation, of course they do. Kacee hears the commotion and runs out of her room yelling.

"No, this isn't fair! He's the creep, why are you arresting her?"

Tears pouring down her face, I squeeze her against me and hold her while she cries. "I'm so sorry, Mommy. This is all my fault."

"Shhh, I'm going to call Grandma and have her come over. Stay here with your brother and get him ready for school. Tell him I had to leave early for work and make sure he gets there. I don't want him at the police station." I grab her face and make her look at me. "Stop crying, baby, we'll get this all sorted out and I'll be home soon."

I swallow the guilt knowing I just lied to my daughter. I know they aren't going to release me anytime soon. I don't have any money or power and they do.

"I'm sorry, ma'am, but we have to handcuff you. You might want to get that call taken care of."

I nod my head and walk with Kacee plastered against my side to the phone. Mom picks up on the first ring sounding worried.

People don't usually call before mid-morning unless it's an emergency. I guess this counts as one.

"Hey, Mama, I need you to come over and stay with the kids for a bit. Kacee can explain when you get here."

"I don't understand, what's going on?"

I hear the panic in her voice, but I try to block it out and get off the phone quickly.

"I don't have time to explain, please come over."

"Okay, I'll be there soon."

I hang up, relieved she didn't make me tell her more.

"Okay, baby girl, after you get your brother to school, I need you to tell Grandma what I did then have her find me a lawyer." Her eyes fill with fear; I can imagine how scared she is to retell her story again. "Don't tell her anything but what I did and I'll handle the rest. Ask Mrs. Jennings across the hall to keep Austin when he gets home from school."

I wait for her nod before I step away and hold out my wrists to the police. Their remorseful faces help make this a little easier.

Thank god it's still early and most of the neighbors aren't out yet. I walk quietly to the police car and sit back for the short drive to the station. Looking around, I can't help but be curious about the equipment up front. I wish there wasn't a cage separating me like an animal to be feared. I guess in a way I am; you mess with one of my kids, I am going to come after you.

I'm relieved the police station is mostly empty when we arrive. They process my booking and place me in holding. I haven't said a word other than I am waiting for my lawyer. Two hours I sit on the bench staring at the wall; I'm too scared to think about what is going to happen to the kids if I don't get out. Instead, I sing songs in my head, but by the third round of Maroon 5's "She Will Be Loved" I am ready to climb the walls in frustration. Finally, I hear my mother down the hall yelling at anyone she sees, demanding to see me immediately. One of the cops from this morning comes in with a smirk on his face.

"I'm going to move you to a room so your mother and lawyer can meet with you."

I sag in relief hearing she found a lawyer. I follow meekly down the hall to a small room with a table in the middle and chairs on both sides. I'm surprised there isn't a mirror in here; I've watched so many cop shows I thought that was standard.

Mom is already inside and launches herself at me.

"Brittany, what is going on? They said they are charging you with assault. You've never hurt anyone in your life, this has to be a mistake."

As she speaks, her voice rises higher and higher. I can hear the panic and feel guilt for putting her through another crisis. Why can't I be a good daughter? I shake off my maudlin feelings and turn to the older gentleman standing by the table.

"I sure hope you are my lawyer."

I'm a little concerned at his appearance; he's well past his prime, severely overweight and wearing rumpled clothes. I glance at Mama and she gives me an apologetic shrug. I turn back as he holds his hand out to me. I shake it firmly, ignoring the slimy feeling of his palm.

"My name is Carter Jepsen. Let's talk about what happened and go from there."

In other words, let's find out if your case is worth my time. I sit down and take a deep breath, waiting while they get situated in their chairs. He nods and I start my story.

"I was working at the diner last night when my cell phone started buzzing in my pocket. I was running food and ignored it. When I checked a few minutes later, there were four missed calls, three texts and a voicemail from Kacee. I read the texts first. She said Dirk Montgomery had shown up at 'The Haunt' and was really drunk." I see my mom's eyes widen and Mr. Jepsen's pen pause when I get to Dirk's name. He is obviously considering right then if he should walk away. "Kacee had tried to leave and Dirk wouldn't let her. She had escaped to the bathroom and wanted me to come get her. The voicemail was a sobbing Kacee saying Dirk had attacked her but she had gotten away and was hiding around the corner."

"Why didn't you call the police at that point?"

I give him my best motherly "are you kidding me" look with a quirked eyebrow and tilted head. He clears his throat and has the sense to look sheepish. Everyone in the surrounding area knows the Montgomery's are the most powerful family around. They can pretty much say and do whatever they want with no repercussion. I shake my head and continue on.

"I ran out of there and found her huddling between some cars in the back parking lot. Her shirt was ripped open. I had every intention of taking her home and forgetting about it but when I saw her, I snapped. I put her in the car, locked the doors and stormed in after him." Mama's head is hanging down at this point with tears rolling down her face. I know she is crying for Kacee; I hope none of those tears are because I've shamed her again. "I found him at the bar making out with another girl. I grabbed his shoulder, spun him around and punched as hard as I could. His head snapped back, but he recovered really fast and looked like he was going to hit me so I grabbed a bottle, smashed it against the bar and held it to his throat. I was in a blind rage by that point. I know I screamed some things, but then the bouncers picked me up and tossed me out. I took Kacee home, cleaned her up and put her to bed."

My mother's shoulders are shaking wildly up and down.

"I'm sorry, Mama. I saw her and I couldn't control myself. I know I screwed up again."

Finally, she looks up and I'm shocked into silence. Her tears have turned to laughter she barely contains.

"What I would have given to see you holding a bottle up to that idiot's throat."

"You aren't mad at me?"

"Quite the opposite, I couldn't be prouder. You stood up for your own and there is nothing wrong with that."

The soothing balm of relief flows through my whole body. I didn't realize how worried I was about her reaction till now.

"I know I didn't handle that well..."

Before I can finish my sentence, I yell out in pain. Mama, being proud, had laid her hands over mine and squeezed.

"Ms. Celdonio, have you had your hand looked at since the incident?"

"No, I didn't want to leave Kacee last night. I've been taking pain medicine and babying it the best I could."

"I'm going to have them take you over to the hospital for x-rays, then we'll talk again when you are back."

I take it as a good sign he's still here. He grunts as he stands and waddles over to the door. His knock is immediately answered by the same cop who brought me to the room.

"Hey, Mike, Ms. Celdonio hurt her hand during the incident. Can you run her over to the hospital and get it taken care of?"

"Sure thing, Mr. Jepsen, let me call it in." He turns my way, "I'll be right back to get you."

He smiles as he closes the door. Considering I'm a criminal, I am grateful for the wonderful treatment I'm being given. I know everyone hates the Montgomery family, especially the cops who can't touch them.

"Well, one thing you can be happy about, Dirk turned eighteen last month. At least you didn't assault a minor."

I hadn't even thought of that; this could be so much worse.

"Kacee's out front and she's worried sick. We're going to follow you over to the hospital and she can sit with you while you get taken care of."

The door opens again to my now familiar escort. He shrugs as he holds out the cuffs; I'm grateful that he is being gentle. Mama follows out the hall and squeezes my shoulder as she heads back out front. I'm led out a side door to the waiting police car.

"You should have told us this morning you needed medical attention. We could have taken you to the hospital first."

"I think the adrenaline was still so high, I didn't realize how bad it was till she squeezed it."

He leaned in and buckled me up, whispering in my ear, "Your daughter should be proud of what you did."

I nod and smile sheepishly.

The drive to the hospital is silent. My heartbeat speeds up when I see Kacee standing outside with a nurse and a wheelchair. She looks miserable; I want a do over so badly. I climb in the chair and thank the nurse when she lays a blanket over my handcuffed wrists. As we go inside, I look back and see my escort giving us a lot of space. I guess they really can appreciate what I did.

"I heard you were quite the hero last night. How about we get some x-rays and see if we can't fix you up."

# Chapter Two

## Casey

I stare at the same spot on the ceiling every morning. I watch as it grows brighter with the sunrise, listening to Monica's soft snores beside me. As the room fully illuminates with the morning rays, my alarm beeps quietly. Mechanically, my arm knows exactly where to move to shut it off, my eyes never leaving that boring spot.

I'm the asshole with the perfect job, perfect condo, perfect fiancée, and absolutely no passion for any of them. I sigh and sit up, I'm just being melancholy. Today is the day I write my annual letter to Brittany. People don't know why this day is important to me, they assume someone close to me died, and I don't blame them, in a way it's true. Fifteen years ago, she disappeared; I've never heard a word from her so how do I know she's alive?

Eight years ago, my therapist convinced me to stop looking for her. I did, but I never stopped writing to the only other person in her life I knew, her grandmother. My letters have never been returned so I assume they are making it there. I used to think about flying out there, pictured walking up the sidewalk and finding Brittany sitting on the porch, drinking a sweet tea and holding out her hand like she's been waiting for me to come find her. I try to block those thoughts now.

My therapist says my obsession is unhealthy. He doesn't know about the letters. For all he knows I'm completely over her. Is it a bad sign when you are lying to your therapist?

My thoughts are interrupted by the hand gliding up my back.

"Good morning, love. I'm going to go make you breakfast while you shower."

"Thanks, babe."

I don't even turn and look at her. How can I when I'm sitting here thinking about another woman?

On auto pilot, I get ready for work and kiss Monica's cheek as I sit at the counter to eat. Very little makes it down, the nerves in my stomach are too amped up. Even though I look miserable, I'm not. I love letter day. I lock myself in my office, pull out a piece of heavy paper and my nicest ball point pen, then pour my heart out to Brittany. I recap everything that has happened since I wrote to her last year. I tell her about new restaurants I've tried, places I've travelled. I ask what she's been up to, and how her mom is, then I pack it up and ship it off, never knowing if it gets there. While Monica is in the shower, I yell out my goodbye and head into the office.

This may all sound creepy but I promise it's not. Everyone has convinced me that she must be dead and I can't bear that thought. I'd rather pretend we're long lost pen pals, albeit a very one-sided relationship.

Walking down the hall, I nod at my secretary and head straight for my office. I'm taken aback when I don't hear the click of my door behind me. I turn and find my secretary following me in. She knows what day it is, my calendar is blocked. What is she doing?

"Do you need something, Mrs. Sampson?"

"I'm sorry, sir, I have a bunch of messages for you from a woman desperate to talk to you."

"Give her to someone else, I'm busy today."

"I tried telling her that, but she said you would want to talk to her. She said her name is Maria Celdonio."

My throat instantly goes dry. Fifteen years to the day and Brittany's mom is calling me. They are alive, I always knew it. As the excitement inside me is building, I remember she said the woman was desperate sounding and it's her mom calling, not her. Dread fills my entire body and I collapse into my chair. Maybe she really is gone.

"Sir, are you all right? Can I get you something? Do you want me to have Mr. Marshall call her back?"

I stand and snatch the papers out of her hand.

"No, I need to call her. Can you make sure I'm not disturbed?"

She nods and slips quietly out the door.

I stare at the phone number; after all this time I have a way of contacting them. Once the Internet became available, I spent months looking for them but never found a trace. Right after college this firm hired me, they have a team of private investigators at their disposal. I considered using them many times, but my therapist was right. I was obsessing and I needed to move on. If she wanted to be found, she wouldn't be hiding so well.

I reach a trembling hand to the phone and dial slowly, as if I'm scared it's all a joke and she won't pick up the phone. My stomach clenches when a soft voice picks up on the first ring.

"Hi, my name is Casey Sanders. I'm trying to reach..."

"Casey, thank god you called me back. I know you have a lot of questions," now that she is talking, I recognize Mrs. Celdonio's voice. "I know we took off on you all those years ago and I'm sorry for that, but Brittany needs you. She's in a lot of trouble and I don't think I can help her this time."

I jump out of my chair involuntarily, my body ready for action. Every fiber of my being is pulsing now that I know she is alive.

"What happened, where is she?"

"She's in jail, they won't let me bond her out and her court hearing is tomorrow." Her voice cracks as she continues on, "I don't think they are going to let her out and I don't know what to do."

"Tell me where you are and I can be there today."

Nerves tingle through my body. This torturous mystery will finally be over.

"We're in Salt Lake City, Utah."

A grim look crosses my face. She's in the same city I've been sending those letters to.

Has she been getting them all this time? I'll add that to my list of questions when I see her. "Give me her lawyer's name and I'll get things started while I'm on the plane."

"Well, Carter Jepsen saw her this morning but he hasn't agreed to take her case yet. Honestly, I don't think I'm going to find anyone in the area to help us."

"Why the hell not?" What could she possibly have done to make her case untouchable?

"She pissed off the Montgomery family and they run things around here. Nobody wants to get on their bad side."

I can't help but chuckle, "Of course that wouldn't stop Britt from standing up to them."

"I promise you she did it for the right reasons. If you can forgive us for taking off on you all those years ago, we would be grateful for your help."

"It's not even a question, I'll be there by tonight. As soon as I have my flight information, I will text it to you. Is this your cell phone number?"

"Yes, let me know when you get in and I'll meet you at the jail."

"Sounds good, and Maria, thank you for calling."

I slam the phone down and run out the door.

"Leslie, I have a family emergency and need to take off for a few days. I am going home to pack. I need you to book me the next flight out to Salt Lake City and get me a car and a hotel near the courthouse. Check what the state law is to let me practice out there. Also, look up Carter Jepsen, he's a lawyer out there. Text me his address and phone number."

I wait long enough to see she has written all my instructions down before I bolt out the door. On the drive home, I call Monica. I vaguely tell her an old family friend from high school is in trouble and I need to leave. Like the perfect fiancée she is, she tells me she loves me and says she will miss me.

Forty-five minutes later, I have an email with a detailed travel itinerary, and Mr. Jepsen's number. Best of all, Utah practices Pro Hac Vice so all I need besides some paperwork is a lawyer to sponsor me. Thank god for Leslie and her exceptional organizational skills. I grab my bags and head for the door. Waiting outside is a car service; I really need to give Leslie a raise. The ride gives me time to leave a message for Mr. Jepsen asking him to meet me at the jail tonight. Emotions flood my brain. Leaning against the headrest, I let my mind drift back to the last time I saw her.

*Continue reading on Amazon*